He thought she was a common thief!

"I didn't take the brooch, if that's what you're suggesting." Her lovely eyes met Janus's hard gaze.

"I wish I could believe you," he said.

Someone was approaching, and Janus caught her arm in case she attempted to escape. Then, as Stokes, the butler, walked toward them, Rebecca found herself in Janus's arms, being kissed in a way that no stranger ought to kiss a woman.

"How dare you!" Rebecca cried furiously when freed from his hold. "Try that again and I'll sue you for assault!"

"Quite the little firebrand, aren't you?" Janus drawled silkily. "We're going to have a little talk. And it's up to you whether we reach a suitable conclusion—to our mutual benefit."

Man with Two Faces

Jane Corrie

Harlequin Books

TORONTO • NEW YORK • LOS ANGELES • LONDON
AMSTERDAM • PARIS • SYDNEY • HAMBURG
STOCKHOLM • ATHENS • TOKYO • MILAN

Original hardcover edition published in 1982
by Mills & Boon Limited

ISBN 0-373-02551-3

Harlequin Romance first edition June 1983

CHAPTER ONE

'I WISH,' declared Barbara Basnett vehemently, 'that I'd chosen an easier way to make a living, but I didn't envisage having to put up with a perfectionist, or having to go into the mother hen routine when a shattered chick returns to the roost reduced to tears.' She stared gloomily down at her coffee cup. 'I tell you, Rebecca, if my financial affairs were on a healthier footing I'd tell the wretched man to take his business elsewhere. Not that he'd have any trouble, Jackson's would jump at the chance of taking over.' She sighed loudly, and looked at Rebecca, her brown eyes behind her horn-rimmed spectacles narrowing speculatively. 'There are times when I wish I were like you,' she said wistfully. 'With your looks and experience, I'd stop him dead in his tracks.'

Rebecca Lindsey cast her friend an amused glance. 'Thanks for the compliment, although it could have been better phrased, particularly, the "experience" bit!' she commented dryly.

'You know what I mean,' Barbara said impatiently.' Working among all those gorgeous dons and professors, and scything through their proposals of undying love with a casual "You'll feel better in the morning!" You could handle Janus Leon with a hand tied behind your back!'

'You've been absorbing too many of those romantic novels you're typing for Rosalie Stanton,' Rebecca replied lightly, but with a hint of amusement in her voice. 'Successful, over-opinionated authors are definitely not my scene, in spite of your overrated opinion of my competence, let alone the injustice you're doing to my learned employers. It's not at all like that,' she added indignantly, her lovely sapphire-blue eyes opening wide at her insistence.

'That's not how Dulcie Jeans told it,' Barbara said quickly, 'she came down from Cambridge a fortnight ago, and she's green with envy at the chances she said you'd passed up.' She eyed Rebecca with a look of speculation in her eyes. 'There's a John Sanderson, I believe, son of the celebrated Sir George, who, as well as belonging to one of the most influential political families in the country, has not only inherited his father's brains, but his looks as well,' she gave Rebecca another sly look. 'Not to mention Ralph Hastings, whom I'm sure Dulcie had a definite soft spot for, plus half the girls in her college, and who completely dries up in the middle of a lecture on the Napoleonic Wars if he happens to catch sight of you walking across the square, and what's more, it's apparently his favourite subject—need I say more?' she queried lightly.

The door of Barbara's office was opened suddenly at this point, and the appearance of a tearful girl prevented Rebecca from attempting any clarification of the facts, and Barbara's dismayed, 'Oh, no!' on the abrupt entry of the girl took her mind off her annoyance at being classed as a heartbreaker.

'I want to hand in my notice!' declared the girl, angrily brushing away a stray tear that coursed down her cheek. 'And I'll only stay on if I can be excused from any work of Mr Leon's!' she ended furiously.

Barbara shot Rebecca a look that said, 'What did I tell you?' and taking a deep breath before replying as brightly as she was able to under the somewhat trying circumstances, 'Very well, Jean. I'll put someone else on to his work. Er—how far did you get?' she queried.

The girl gave a sniff and replied in a voice that spoke of relief at attaining her object and keeping her job. 'I finished the ninth chapter. Mirabelle did the eighth, and I think Sandra did the seventh. I'm not sure who did the six——'

'Yes, well, we won't worry about that,' Barbara interceded swiftly with a weary note in her voice. 'You'd better send Linda in to me,' she ordered, and as the girl left the office, she turned to Rebecca. 'You see how it is?' she asked dismally, 'and here's another lamb for the slaughter,' she added under her breath as a slim, pretty girl entered the office.

'You wanted me?' queried Linda, tossing her fair hair back from her face in a movement that spoke of vanity, and in spite of the question Rebecca, idly watching her, felt she was quite sure of the reason behind the summons, and there was a touch of importance in her bearing as she awaited her employer's orders.

'How far have you got with *Passionate Night*?' Barbara asked the girl.

'Oh, I ought to be through with it by this afternoon,' the girl replied brightly, and waited expectantly.

There was a short pause while Barbara studied her, then she gave her a quick smile. 'So I can tell her she can have it tomorrow, then,' she said. 'All right, Linda, thank you,' and she dismissed the puzzled-looking girl.

Rebecca's brows lifted in query as the door closed behind her, but she made no comment, and her thoughts returned to that rather unfair accusation Barbara had levelled against her earlier, making her sound like the college flirt, but she decided against making an issue of it. 'How's Dulcie making out?' she asked casually. 'I haven't seen her since she left college. Did she get that job she was after?'

Barbara gave a noncommittal grunt that showed her thoughts were far away from college affairs. 'Who can I send him now?' she said worriedly, addressing her question to the room at large as if seeking inspiration from the office furnishings.

As the question had not been directed at Rebecca, she did not attempt to give a reply, not that she could have done anyway, as apart from the fact that her friend ran a typing agency, she knew nothing of the actual running of the business.

At this point the telephone on Barbara's desk shrilled out an imperious command, and with her thoughts still on her problem she reached out for the receiver with a mechanical action. 'Basnett Typing Agency,' she said, then as she listened to the voice on the other end of the line, drew in a quick breath before saying stiffly, 'Of course, Mr Leon. We shall do our best, although I'm not sure about tomorrow——' There was a short pause while she listened to the reply, and her lips straightened in fury before she replied, 'Very well. Tomorrow,' and slammed the receiver down on its rest, then sat staring at the top of her desk, before saying wearily, 'So it will have to be Linda. Damn the man!'

Rebecca glanced at her watch. She was due at the British Museum at twelve to pick up some data for Professor Donan, and she had to remember to call in at the Oxford Street bookshop to collect the book they'd promised to get for Bill Harper, and the way things were going for Barbara that morning, she would cope better without distraction. Taking a hasty swallow of the last of her coffee, she drew her handbag towards her in preparation for her departure. 'I'll leave you to get on with your work,' she said, with a smile of sympathy. 'I've got to get to the Museum before twelve. Anything you want me to pick up for a meal tonight—or will we be eating out?' she asked her friend.

Barbara shook her head as if to clear the fog that had descended around her and made an attempt to concentrate her thoughts elsewhere. 'Oh, I thought we might eat out,' she replied vaguely, then as Rebecca got up to leave suddenly asked her, 'What did you think of Linda?'

Rebecca's fine brows rose at the question. 'I can hardly pass an opinion,' she replied lightly, 'not on such a short showing,' she added, as she walked towards the door. 'I'll think about it, but she looked capable to me. Anyway, I must get going,' as she cast another quick glance at her watch.

'Blast the Museum!' Barbara said explosively. 'Why can't they do their own shopping? And why on earth should they expect you to do it during your vacation? Let alone have to go to the trouble of posting the stuff off to them. Here I am, in the devil of a hole, and all you can do is mutter about doing a few errands! Look, I'll send one of the girls to collect the stuff for you, and do any other shopping you want done. What I want you to do is use that cool brain of yours and see if we can't come up with a solution, because if we can't, I shall lose the Agency,' she added dismally.

Rebecca turned from the door and walked back slowly towards the desk again. 'Lose the Agency?' she echoed with a hint of disbelief in her voice. 'But you said you were doing fine,' she added accusingly, 'and it didn't look as if you were short of work when I came in. The clatter of typing out there proves that. It's a positive hive of activity!'

Barbara sighed loudly, and pointed towards the chair that Rebecca had just left. 'Appearances,' she said slowly, 'can be deceptive.' Then she gave a shrug. 'Oh, well, I might as well come clean. I've had my eye on some new offices for some time now, and two weeks ago they became vacant.' She took a deep breath. 'So I took a gamble and put a deposit on them before they were snapped up by someone else. Getting Janus Leon's work was the turning point for me—at least I thought it was,' she added with a sigh. 'He's such a big name, you see, and it was bound to bring in more business for me. What I didn't take into account was that not one of my staff came up to his high standards, and the more the wretched man bullies them, the worse they get. They're positively terrified of him, and shrink down on their chairs trying to look frantically busy each time another casualty slinks back to the bureau.'

She pressed a bell on her desk, and when the summons was answered by one of the girls, she requested that Ann should be sent round to the British Museum, and got Rebecca to write down the name of the Professor and the data to be collected. The book she had promised to pick up for Bill Harper could wait, Rebecca decided, and she shook her head when asked if there was anything else she wanted done.

With that out of the way, Barbara settled down to her problems again. 'It wouldn't be so bad,' she went on, 'if he'd send the work in to the bureau, but no, he insists on having the work done at his place, which at the moment is in an hotel, where he occupies a suite until he decides whether to settle down here, or go back to Australia. At least, that was the inference I got from the blurb of one of his books. I just can't afford to lose his business now,' she wailed. 'I'm only existing on a shoestring at the moment. All the capital I have in the world is tied up in the new offices.' She gave a shrug. 'I would have to move anyway, in time, this whole block's been taken over by a cash-and-carry store and it would be just a question of time before they gave us notice to quit,' she added dolefully.

Rebecca sent her friend a sympathetic look, but

apart from that did not see what other help she could give her. 'What about this Linda?' she suggested hopefully. 'She didn't look the type to be cowed. If she's at all competent she ought to manage, and it did look as if she was hoping for the assignment.'

'Linda,' Barbara announced with an ironic note in her voice, 'is a fool. Oh, she's competent enough. She's also nice looking, and she knows it.' She screwed up her eyes. 'I can see her now, tossing those fair locks of hers back in what she thinks is a provocative come-on, not to mention fluttering her eyelashes at what she deemed to be the appropriate moment.' She gave a heavy sigh. 'Linda,' she said sourly, 'wouldn't last a day. Janus Leon has the reputation of being a playboy, but he doesn't believe in mixing business with pleasure, as our Linda will soon find out. Besides that, models and society butterflies are more his line of country, he wouldn't lower his standards where a small-town typist was concerned.'

'Well, can't you give her a hint on those lines?' Rebecca suggested.

'Can you see her listening?' Barbara replied dryly, 'because I can't, so I might as well save my breath, and keep the girl in the bureau. She's a good worker, as long as there are no distractions.'

There was a heavy silence after this, then Rebecca said, 'Well, if there's no one else to send, it looks as if you'll have to risk it.'

Her friend did not seem to have heard her. 'One week,' she said musingly. 'That's all I want,' then she gazed speculatingly at Rebecca.

Rebecca returned her look with a trace of puzzlement in her lovely eyes. She was to remember afterwards that she ought to have seen it coming; she was very fond of Barbara, but she had a nasty habit of organising other people's lives, particularly when it concerned good causes, and this good cause was decidedly nearer to home than any of the others had been.

'You're not due in Berkshire until the eighteenth, are you?' she asked Rebecca with a gleam in her eye, then looked down at her desk quickly as she saw the look of wariness that appeared somewhat belatedly in the other girl's eyes.

'I haven't made up my mind to accept John's invitation yet,' Rebecca replied slowly, then added hastily, 'and if you're thinking what I think you're thinking, it's no go—but definitely no go! I want a rest, not a wrestling match with an overflated egoist.'

'Who said anything about a wrestling match?' Barbara queried with a look of innocent indignation in her voice, but she did not fool Rebecca. 'Look, it's just a straightforward job of audio-typing—kid's play to you. No dictation to worry about, not personal dictation, it's all on tape. The only thing you'll have to put up with is the wretched man hovering over you for the first day or so, to make sure you don't ruin his precious novel. I shouldn't think he'd bother you after the first ten minutes, once he's seen your capabilities.' She shot Rebecca a pleading look. 'Please, Rebecca. It's only for one week, and it will keep the pot boiling until Margaret Morton joins us.'

Rebecca threw her a dark look. 'Just for the record,' she said dryly, 'what if this Margaret whatnot can't make it—or has 'flu or some other indisposition that prevents her from taking over— I presume you've thought of that, because if you haven't I'd advise you to start thinking now. If I take over, and it's a big if,' she said warningly, at Barbara's swift sigh of relief as if it were already settled, 'it will only be for a week, and then only to oblige you, but if he starts any funny business, then I'm off. I have enough to put up with at college and don't intend to spend my vacation being chased round an office desk—not for you or for anyone!' she declared vehemently.

'I've told you, you've nothing to worry about in that direction,' Barbara replied soothingly, 'and not in the other either. Margaret won't let me down, she's a personal friend and utterly reliable. After spending twenty-five years as a court stenographer, she's more than ready for a less hectic post. I'd like to see Mr Janus Leon try to bully Margaret, she'd flatten him with one look, *and* have his work ready for him before he could turn round,' she added, with a note of satisfaction in her voice.

By the time the girls had had lunch at a nearby café, everything was settled, and Rebecca was scolding herself for letting herself be talked into doing something that she didn't want to do. She was too soft, that was her trouble, and it was as well for her that she was able to draw the line where affairs of the heart were concerned, and skilfully sidestep any embroilment in that line.

To the casual observer this attitude had produced a certain amount of speculation. That she was heartless was one label given her. Too proud was another, and failing any other explanation, that she was desperately in love with a man who was not free to marry her.

In all fairness, Rebecca did not qualify for any of them, unless her view of not accepting any invitations from a man she was unable to feel anything for, apart from friendship, qualified her for the 'heartless' title, in which case she was guilty.

Now, at twenty-two years of age, Rebecca had never been in love. She had been the only child of divorced parents, and had spent her early childhood being used as a pawn on the chessboard of misguided parenthood, and could only call her life her own on the decease of her one surviving parent when she was eighteen, and she had often wondered if her early upbringing had soured her expectations in the matrimonial lucky dip, for that was how she looked on it. Her mother had so often remarked with a self-pitying sigh, 'If only I'd had married dear Tony—but no, I wouldn't listen to my mother. I had to marry your father.' Rebecca had privately thought that there was no 'had to' about it. She had married her father because she had wanted to marry him, and that was all there was to it.

In spite of the emotional gambits that had surrounded her early childhood, Rebecca had been fond of both her parents. She had learnt at an early stage how to combat each bitter tirade levelled at the absent partner, but had at times felt a little sorry for her mother, for there was no doubt that her father had a roving eye, and his handsome features and smooth manner had assured him of success wherever his attention had strayed.

Rebecca had inherited her father's good looks and his colouring. Her lovely red-gold hair and wide sapphire-blue eyes framed in a heart-shaped face, with high cheekbones and delicate aristocratic nose, that had a habit of wrinkling in censorious fashion if she was displeased, had earned her the nickname of 'Duchess' among her companions.

If she had spared herself the time to analyse her feelings where romance was concerned, she would have had to admit that the past had left its mark on her. Deep down she was terrified of involvement of any kind, but as yet that fear had not been put to the test. No man had attracted her attention, not in matters of the heart, and her obstinate refusal to take any besotted male seriously was, in her view, completely justified, for she did not encourage such devotion, only sheer perversity made them determined to storm the battlements. It had become a kind of game, and she knew that bets had been made on likely candidates, and this did not only include the teaching staff, but had permeated through to the students, who had cheerfully directed their energies away from the crowning of the central college spire with an unmentionable object to the melting of the snows within the breast of the Bursar's secretary.

Had the students been younger, Rebecca's life would have been a great deal easier, but as most of them were around her own age, and in some cases older, it was particularly trying for her, and there were times when she had seriously considered joining her friend Barbara in the Agency. So far she had managed to cope, and the fact that she loved her job, was competent, and saw no reason why she should be forced to leave for such, in her mind, utterly senseless reasons, made her even more unapproachable.

The end-of-term holidays also brought their crop of delicate sidestepping away from any involvement during the break with any member of staff, and innocent-sounding queries on what she intended to do with her time off period were met with equally vague-sounding replies. It was generally known that she spent part of her vacation with her friend in London, hence the two small errands she had undertaken to do for members of staff, but apart from that, her plans were kept to herself. Sometimes Barbara would take a week off from the Agency, even a fortnight, if things were slack, but Rebecca was never at a loss for entertainment. Many invitations were issued to her, but she accepted only those that ensured her freedom from involvement with a member of staff, or indeed anyone connected with the College.

This year, however, she had decided to break the golden rule, and accept John Sanderson's ritual offer of a fortnight at his home in Berkshire. There were two reasons why she had broken the rules she had strictly adhered to in the past—one was that Sir George Sanderson's gatherings at his country seat always consisted of large parties. He didn't believe in doing things by half, and Rebecca could count on at least a dozen guests being included in the party, and as far as she was concerned there was safety in numbers.

The second reason was that she knew the family through their daughter Laura, whom she had been at school with, and had retained the friendship even though Rebecca was now a working girl, and Laura a socialite, of whom nothing was expected other than that she make a good marriage, preferably with some young up-and coming politician.

It had been a plea from Laura that had made her decide to accept the invitation. 'I haven't seen you for ages,' she had written, and, 'For goodness' sake come and rescue me. I shall die of boredom if you don't!'

The note had made Rebecca smile, it was so characteristic of Laura, and she wondered how her father had got her to stay on for the house party, for Rebecca knew she made a point of avoiding them like the plague. She loathed intellectual gatherings, and as she had once said to Rebecca, 'Having suffered a surfeit of them in my youth, I have no intention of putting up with them now. I shall probably marry a farmer who hates politicians and loves pigs. I'm quite fond of them myself, actually,' she had added with a wistful note in her voice.

To be absolutely honest with herself, Rebecca was quite looking forward to the house party, and knew full well that the chances were that she would be urged to stay on for another week or so after the other guests had gone, and she was not averse to this. A few weeks' cosseting in the bosom of the very wealthy would come as a welcome break from the hard, if enjoyable, daily work routine. Breakfast in bed, if she so desired it, days of lolling about on the spacious lawns of Pinehurst. Tea taken in a shaded arbour, and nothing to worry about except dressing for dinner, and even that was not strictly adhered to. Sir George's guests were more concerned with the state of the country than with the vagaries of fashion.

With Laura present, Rebecca knew she would be able to counteract any well-laid scheme thought up by her brother to inveigle her into accepting his proposal. It was not so much that Laura thought her brother dull, but that she was very fond of Rebecca, and had once warned her, 'Don't get involved with John. I know he's good-looking, but honestly, he's a Sanderson through and through. He'll smother you, and you won't be able to call your life your own—and besides, I'll never forgive you,' she had added with a twinkle in her eye.

All this went through Rebecca's mind as she unpacked her suitcase in the spare bedroom in Barbara's flat. Barbara had gone back to the bureau after lunch in high spirits, certain that her worries had been solved, and leaving Rebecca feeling intensely annoyed with herself for having been talked into taking on such a task and having to spend the first week of her well-earned holiday in the company of what sounded like a thoroughly disagreeable man.

When she reached the end of her unpacking and hung up the last dress in the wardrobe, she wondered vaguely what she should wear for duty the following day. She had not envisaged herself sitting at an office desk and typing reams—she stopped in thought; what sort of stories did Janus Leon write? she wondered, and wished she had read one of them. She would then be prepared for whatever literary treat lay in store for her. She frowned. She hoped it was literary, and not one of the more lurid representations of the art. She gave a slight shudder. If Barbara had let her in for that, she would never forgive her! In which case, Margaret Morton would just have to join the bureau a little sooner than anticipated!

Her eyes then fell upon her blue woollen dress. It was absolutely plain and of a soft sea-blue, and a particular favourite of hers, but not a dress for office wear, for in spite of its simplicity it was elegant, and like most of Rebecca's clothes was expensive, and chosen with care for long-range use. She had inherited a small legacy from her father, but with the future in mind, she had drawn frugally from this account, and usually saved some of her salary to pay for the more expensive items in her wardrobe.

After another quick survey of her wardrobe, she had to settle for the blue. There was nothing else she could possibly wear. She had packed with the intention of getting a tan in the shortest possible time, and her other dresses were either halter-tops or light summery concoctions suitable for lounging about on the lawns of Pinehurst, but would still look eminently respectable for tea in the drawing-room if the weather turned against them.

After the girls had dined out that evening, they

returned to the flat for a cosy evening of chat, and
Rebecca was able to satisfy her curiosity about
Janus Leon's work in order to prepare herself for
the morrow.

On her query, Barbara expressed surprise that
Rebecca had not heard of the celebrated author.
'He writes adventure-cum-detective stories, all set
in the Australian bush. His backgrounds are
authentic, of course. I did tell you that he's an
Australian, didn't I?' she asked the partially
relieved Rebecca, who began to feel that it mightn't
be so bad after all; at least her earlier fears had
been laid to rest. 'Unlike other authors, he didn't
need to go abroad to make his name,' continued
Barbara, 'he's just as popular in his own country
as he is here.' She gave Rebecca a wry smile. 'You
know, it just shows how shut off you become in
that university of yours,' she wagged her head
impishly at her. 'You know what they say about
too much learning,' she teased Rebecca lightly.

'Oh, bosh!' Rebecca replied with a grin. 'It suits
me, anyway,' then she stared at her slim sandalled
feet. 'Although,' she conceded slowly, 'I must
admit you have a point there, outside events rarely
intrude upon our hallowed existence—not that I
want them to,' she added quickly, 'but it is another
world.'

'There you are, then,' Barbara answered knowingly, 'and if you don't watch out, life will have
passed you by. I can see you now,' she went on
warningly, but the twinkle in her eye belied her
words, 'with that glorious hair speckled with grey,
and twisted into a hideous bun.' Her eyes swept

over Rebecca's slight figure. 'You're just right now, but you'll get plumper with all that sitting about you do. You'll probably end up making history by becoming the first woman bursar——' At this point she had to duck hastily to avoid the cushion Rebecca hurled at her.

Before Rebecca fell asleep that night, her thoughts went back over Barbara's words. She knew she had only been teasing her, but her light-hearted prediction had not been all that far off the mark, and it had echoed Rebecca's own thoughts on the matter.

There was no doubt about it, she thought drowsily before she fell asleep. She would have to make a move one day out of the cloying but eminently satisfying atmosphere of university life. If she didn't, Barbara's prediction would almost certainly come true.

CHAPTER TWO

THE following morning Rebecca made her not very enthusiastic way to the Royal Victoria, a small but very exclusive hotel in a secluded square in Mayfair, and after being given a very close scrutiny by the desk clerk before he informed their celebrated guest that a secretary had arrived, and requesting permission to send her up, Rebecca found herself in the lift and being borne towards her destination.

Her first impression of Janus Leon was of a tall and ruggedly handsome man. His brown hair made no concession to fashion and was cut fairly short, a welcome change for Rebecca after the somewhat mixed batch of styles of the college students. But it was his eyes that held the attention. She had never seen eyes of such a piercing blue and that seemed to look right through her, although he had only seemed to glance at her before striding through to the bedroom that was being used as an office, and leaving Rebecca to follow after him feeling like something that had inadvertently wandered into his domain and must now be put to good use.

His voice was low and resonant, with a pure English accent, and Rebecca knew a spurt of surprise, for she had not unnaturally expected an Australian accent. 'I think you'll find everything you need,' he said, as he nodded towards a desk placed against the window to gain as much light as was possible, and then subjected her to a hard brief impersonal scrutiny, his blue gaze narrowing as he took in her dress after she had taken her light raincoat off in preparation to starting work. 'You do know how to manage these machines, don't you?' he asked suspiciously, 'because if you don't, say so now—I've wasted enough time lately on so-called secretarial help.'

Rebecca's fine eyebrows went up at this rather uncalled-for condemnation of Barbara's staff, and she was in complete sympathy with those who had failed to come up to his exacting standards. The wretched man had only himself to blame. Had he been more understanding, he would have got better

results. Bullying tactics never worked and in-
variably produced mistakes, and she wondered why
he used an agency in the first place. A man as successful as he was supposed to be ought to have a
private secretary, only she couldn't imagine anyone
taking the job on. Good secretaries were never at a
loss for work and didn't have to join the slave trade
to make a living.

All this went through her mind as her eyes met
his fierce blue stare. 'I do not envisage any problems,' she said quietly, in the tone of voice that
spoke of capability. 'If you would just leave things
to me and let me get on in my own time, I think
you will find my work satisfactory,' she ended,
indicating plainly that she saw no reason for his
presence, particularly if he meant to take such a
belligerent attitude.

The thin line of his firm lips showed Rebecca
that he had got the message and did not like it at
all. He was not used to someone else taking the
initiative. 'I take it you won't mind if I occasionally
look in on you, will you?' he asked sarcastically. 'I
know miracles sometimes happen, but you must
forgive my scepticism. You don't,' he added meaningly, 'look the part,' his gaze wandered over her
expensive dress, 'and if you're as capable as you
apparently seem to think you are, then what the
devil are you doing in an agency? Or are you only
working for pin money?' His gaze went straight to
her hands now resting on the top of the desk
patiently waiting to start work, and Rebecca knew
he was looking for a wedding ring. Many young
married women took on agency work because it

did not tie them to regular hours as a permanent job did. 'Not married, or engaged, I see,' he commented.

Rebecca had no intention of entering upon any personal conversation with him, and she highly resented his insolence. She knew he was baiting her. She had annoyed him, and he was getting his own back—it was as simple as that, but she was not going to give him the satisfaction of knowing he had annoyed her. She counteracted this by giving him a sweet synthetic smile; she had had plenty of practice in dealing with this type of situation in the past and it held her in good stead now. 'I understood from Miss Basnett that you like two carbons,' she said sweetly, as she selected two sheets of copy paper and then put the carbons between them, and with the same slow deliberation placed the thicker sheet on top and put them in the typewriter, then without even glancing at him, switched on the dictating machine.

When she next glanced up, she saw that he had gone, but even after his departure she could still feel the rapier glance he had thrown her before he left her to get on with the work. It was as well, she thought lightly, that she was competent, and that Barbara had given her a good grounding on how it should be set out, although she had the rest of the manuscript to use as a guide had she been in any doubt, for there was no doubt that she had made an enemy of Janus Leon, who simply was not used to finding himself on the wrong end of an exchange of personalities.

It was also as well, she thought darkly, that she

had had previous experience in preparing work for publication, although that had consisted of various theses submitted by the dons to further the cause of education.

By the end of the morning, Rebecca was well into the tenth chapter, and had not even noticed the passing of time. A tray of coffee had been brought in to her around ten-thirty, by a member of the hotel staff, and this had surprised her, for she could not see the sarcastic Janus Leon ordering her any refreshment, but evidently someone had, and although she did not take a break at this time, she drank the coffee while she worked, a practice that was normal to her during work at the college.

Whatever else Janus Leon was, there was no denying his skill as a writer, and Rebecca was fair enough to acknowledge this salient fact, and was soon caught up in the story as it unfolded into the written word on the typescript before her.

As her previous work in this field had been purely of a scholastic nature, she found the work eminently satisfying, and thought with a slight pang of depression that she would find her old job even more of a dull chore when she returned to it, but cheered herself up with the thought of at least having a good relationship with her superiors who were almost apologetic when giving her what were, after all was said and done, her normal duties.

She saw no more of Janus Leon that morning, and considered this a victory. It only needed a firm hand, she told herself, and the experience to deal with that type of bullying man.

When she returned from lunch, however, she

found to her annoyance that although he had made a point of keeping his distance, he had kept a wary eye on her work, for she found two more tapes on her desk, and a message to the effect that if an Alan Sinclair rang up she was to ask him to call on Mr Leon at ten the following day.

Rebecca's lips folded in annoyance as she read this cryptic message, noting that he had not added a 'thank you' for doing work other than that she had been taken on to do. Answering the telephone and making appointments came under the duties of a private secretary, and what if this Sinclair person couldn't make the stated time? Was she expected to hunt around for his personal diary and suggest another time? She intended to do nothing of the sort. She was there to type his novel, and couldn't be expected to get on with her work if she had to chase around on other duties. If the time was unsuitable she would ask the man to ring back again and have a word with Janus Leon.

In the event the man did not ring, but several other people did, and an annoyed Rebecca was forced to answer each call in the expectation of it being Alan Sinclair. On each occasion she requested the caller to ring again that evening in the hope of catching what was turning out to be her elusive boss, and it did occur to her that perhaps his absence was a deliberate act on his part to cause her annoyance, and she would certainly have to have a stern word with him on this point, if she ever saw him before the end of her week. It was either that, or just let the phone ring and get on with the work she was supposed to be doing.

The following day, Rebecca's hopes of a week free from the annoying presence of Janus Leon took a decided setback as he was waiting for her in the office as soon as she walked in, and her 'good morning,' given more in the line of protocol than an actual cheery greeting, met with a grunt that she supposed was a reciprocal reply.

'Did Alan ring?' he asked abruptly, as Rebecca took off her coat and walked over to her desk.

'Mr Sinclair did not ring,' she replied coolly. 'There were several other calls. I presume they rang back last night,' she added firmly, 'I told them to, anyway.'

His black winged brows shot up at her reply and indirect meaning that he could not have failed to interpret. His lips thinned as he said brusquely, 'So I found out. The wretched phone kept me busy for the better part of the evening. You are a secretarial agency, aren't you?' he shot out at her accusingly. 'I should have thought that was part of your chores.'

Rebecca gave him a cool stare. 'It depends,' she said carefully, 'which you consider more important—your novel, or the secretarial work. The amount of calls put through yesterday afternoon, that continually held me up, makes it necessary to get a ruling on this,' and giving a light shrug that showed that she had no preference in the matter whatsoever, and that it was entirely up to him, she sat waiting for his reply.

That she had annoyed him was patently obvious by the sudden blaze of fury in his startlingly blue eyes, before he gave her a slow and, to Rebecca's way of thinking, insolent appraisal, his gaze resting finally on her smooth features. 'What happened to the "service with a smile" slogan?' he queried sarcastically. 'As you're so competent, I shouldn't have thought a few phone calls would have upset you.'

'It was more than a few calls,' Rebecca snapped back, and immediately regretted losing her temper. It was she now who was bringing personalities into it. She didn't like the man, but he was an important client of Barbara's. 'Look,' she said quietly, willing herself not to show her feelings, 'it's not that I mind what I do, but if you want me to take on the secretarial work as well, I would have to have your diary, and have some idea of your movements, wouldn't I? and as I've just said, it does hold me up on the other work.' She gave a light shrug. 'Perhaps if you employed a secretary specifically for this work it might help,' she suggested calmly, as she drew the typewriter towards her in preparation for starting work.

'Asking for the job, are you?' he queried insolently.

Rebecca's brows raised. What an obnoxious man he was! 'Er—no, thank you!' she replied with more emphasis than was really necessary, and added quickly, 'Agency work suits me,' and fed paper into the machine in an effort to prevent further discussion on this theme.

'That's just as well,' he replied thinly, before he stamped out of the room. 'I'd want a more flexible type.'

Rebecca glared at the door he had just closed

behind him. Well, at least she had got that straight! The phone could ring all morning for all she cared, after a remark like that he could hardly expect her to oblige!

As if to test her resolution, the telephone rang shortly after this, but she worked stolidly on, completely ignoring its imperative ring. A few seconds later there was silence and she presumed that Janus Leon had answered it, and with a small nod of satisfaction she got on with her work.

Two days later, Rebecca gazed out of the bedroom-cum-office window and on to the street below. The impatient hooting of a taxi as it tried to bypass another that was just drawing up in front of the hotel went unnoticed by her. She saw only acres of paddocks where sheep grazed, and an old homestead built of red brick, with its kitchen garden and immaculately lawned frontage that presided over the surrounding buildings housing the staff that ran the huge sheep station.

Her lips softened into a smile at the thought that she would know the place in the story anywhere, should she ever see it. She would even recognise the characters portrayed, for she was sure they had been drawn from real people. The thought jerked her out of her reverie. What on earth was the matter with her? It was only a story after all, a figment of the author's imagination, she didn't suppose such a place existed, and even if it did, she would certainly never see it, yet as she took the last sheet of paper out of the typewriter, she had a sudden presentiment that one day she would see

the homestead, and gave a quick sigh of exasperation at her foolishness. She had obviously been
overworking!

As she neatly stacked the finished sheets together, she became aware of Janus Leon standing
by the door silently watching her, and she
wondered how long he had been there, and whether
he had witnessed her lapse of concentration as she
went into her reverie. Not that it mattered much if
he had, she thought musingly; she had finished the
tape and the story. He could have no complaints.

She watched his measured tread as he came towards her desk, his hard blue gaze on the sheets of
typescript that she was now assembling in numer-
ical order.

'Was that the last chapter?' he asked with a note
of incredulity in his voice, and at Rebecca's nod of
confirmation he frowned, and picked up the
chapter she was about to attach to the rest of the
manuscript.

Rebecca's eyes followed the lines of the long lean
hand that held the typescript, and from there went
to his hard features as he closely studied the result
of her work, giving each page minute scrutiny. She
was certain that although he had not bothered her
during the day, but had kept his distance, he had
closely studied each day's progress and would have
pounced on any mistake with the ferocity of a tiger,
and thoroughly enjoyed giving her a set-down. She
saw the way his dark brows went up, as he reached
the end of the chapter, and then looked back at
her. 'Not bad,' he said grudgingly, and that,
Rebecca knew, was as far as he would go in the

praise line. She thought angrily that not only had she finished the work in half the time normally taken, but she had made a good job of it, even if she did say so herself, particularly after what she had seen of the previous chapters with their constant crossings out, and what must have been, from Janus Leon's impeccable standards, inexcusable stupid typing errors, yet all he had said was, 'Not bad'!

'Disappointed, Mr Leon?' she drawled, her annoyance getting the better of common sense, but as his hard eyes bored into hers, she immediately regretted her words.

'Just surprised, Miss Lindsey,' he drawled back at her with an emphasis on the 'Miss' that plainly put Rebecca in her place in case she was attempting any familiarity, and making her want to slap his arrogant face. 'I'm afraid your pace is too good for me,' he went on smoothly. 'I'm only working on the bones of the next story as yet.'

Rebecca managed to stop herself giving a sigh of relief. He hadn't any more work on hand and she was going to be told to go back to the Agency. Her lovely dark blue eyes held a look of innocent query that successfully masked her thoughts, but she was already packing for her stay at Pinehurst.

'Are you still with me, Miss Lindsey?' came a gentle, if sarcastic, query from Janus Leon that brought her back from Sir Geoffrey's country seat to the confines of the office.

'Oh, yes, absolutely!' Rebecca replied quickly. 'I quite understand,' she gave the sardonic man now closely watching her a brilliant smile. 'You've no more work on hand at present, so I'll just finish off the title page for you, and then I'm off,' she ended with a rush of thankfulness.

'Got something on, have you?' he asked casually, and Rebecca stared at him. What on earth did he mean by that? she wondered. He couldn't possibly know—she blinked as she suddenly caught his meaning. Was there some other work she had to do for the Agency? that was what he meant.

'Oh, yes!' she said quickly, adding for Barbara's benefit, 'We're terribly busy, there'll be something lined up for me when I get back,' she lied unblushingly.

'That's just too bad,' he drawled, without a trace of sympathy. 'I'm claiming your services. Whatever's waiting will have to wait.'

Rebecca stared at him with her head on one side, the glorious red tints in her hair catching the light from the window behind her giving an autumn halo that framed her lovely features. 'I beg your pardon?' she replied with a puzzled air, desperately hoping that she had misread his meaning, for if he meant what she thought he meant, then she would lose more of her vacation.

Janus Leon gave a grin that she could only describe as wolfish. 'I'm the first in the queue,' he said. 'Priority claim to your services, in other words,' and before the indignant Rebecca could come up with some excuse as why she had to get back to the Agency, he shot out at her, 'Have you read the manuscript right through?'

Rebecca blinked. Drat the man! Did he want to hear her enthusing about it? There was no denying that he was an excellent writer, but she was certainly not going to add fuel to his overrated ego by saying so! 'Er—no,' she replied slowly, her eyes wary as she waited for the next question.

He bent down to the desk and thrust the manuscript towards her. 'Read it!' he commanded. 'You'll no doubt see what a mess the earlier typists made of it. I want you to retype the worst bits. Any questions?' he barked out at her as, speechless, she tried to calculate how long this would take her, for it meant practically re-doing the first half of the novel. Her lips clamped together in annoyance as the thought occurred to her that he had only himself to blame for bullying the girls; if he'd left them to get on with the work he would have had no complaints. There was nothing like having a Big Brother hovering in the background ready to pounce on any little error and making a girl nervous, it not only destroyed confidence, but almost certainly guaranteed further mistakes.

Her eyes left his narrowed gaze and rested on the manuscript, but her brain was working overtime searching for a way out of this latest setback to her holiday plans. 'I'm afraid I shall have to see Miss Basnett about that,' she said carefully, keeping her eyes on the desk. 'You see, that's straightforward typing, and I'm a stenographer. We have several excellent copy typists in the Agency, but we're rather short of stenographers. Besides,' she added brightly, 'copy typists' rates are lower. I'll have a word with Miss Basnett at lunch time for you,' she said helpfully, congratulating herself on her quick thinking.

'If the first three idiots Miss Basnett sent me are
anything to go by, I'm not risking it,' Janus Leon
replied grimly. 'I don't remember complaining
about the rates,' he added furiously. 'That's my
business. By the time you've got that lot straightened out,' he gave a curt nod towards the manuscript, 'I'll have the first two chapters of the next
novel ready for you. Your work is satisfactory, and
that's all I'm concerned about.'

Rebecca's eyes grew round in consternation.
Next novel! She didn't like the sound of that at all.
Why on earth had she to make such a good job of
the last few chapters? Why hadn't she made a mess
of them? She sighed inwardly. Because she took a
pride in her work, that was why, and because she
hadn't allowed this autocratic male to bully her!
And lastly but not least, she hadn't wanted to let
Barbara down.

'I didn't argue,' she told Barbara later that day.
'It wouldn't have done any good if I had. He
claimed what he called "priority rights" on me,'
and at Barbara's amused chuckle, she added wasp-
ishly, 'Well, I only hope your friend Margaret
comes up to scratch, because I'm off to Berkshire
on Sunday, no matter what!'

'Of course you are, dear,' Barbara replied soothingly. 'I said a week, and that's all I wanted from
you, and I'm very grateful, especially as you've
finished the novel. Just keep him happy for a
couple more days and then Margaret can take over.
I'll say you're off sick if he cuts up rough, although
once he sees Margaret's work we'll have nothing
to worry about.'

CHAPTER THREE

REBECCA breathed in a sigh of pure contentment. She had certainly done the right thing in accepting John's invitation. Not that she wanted to spend all her time being waited on and listening to Laura's humorous, if slightly querulous, complaints about her father's choice of house guest during what he termed his 'open house season'.

She moved the shoulder-strap of her sundress a little farther along in order to get a smooth tan along her shoulders. She could see Laura's point of view, of course, for apart from herself and John, Laura's brother, the rest of the assembly were, as Laura had caustically put it, 'in their dotage', and although this was not strictly true, they were certainly on the wrong side of forty.

As the high-pitched, slightly girlish voice of Mrs Carmichael floated across the pleasantly warm afternoon towards Rebecca, she gave a grin, envisaging that lady's reaction towards that last thought of hers. You could do a lot with beauty aids these days, but you couldn't eradicate time. Laura's scornful, 'I was at school with her daughter,' soon put paid to any pretensions on those lines, and had also put paid to Mrs Carmichael's hopes of becoming Laura's stepmother by outrightly declaring to her father that she couldn't stand the woman, and advising him to take a good hard look at her before committing himself in any way. He had taken Laura's advice. She might be outspoken, but she had an uncanny habit of hitting the nail on the head with unswerving accuracy.

From what Rebecca had seen of Mrs Carmichael, she was of the opinion that Laura's caustic comments had been perfectly justified, and that she had saved her father from making a ghastly mistake. Mrs Carmichael was an odious woman, and her fluffy, little woman act that dispersed into resentment in a younger, attractive woman's presence the minute the men were out of earshot gave one no illusions as to her true character.

It had not taken Mrs Carmichael long to size up the situation as one after another of her well-laid schemes went sadly astray, and she knew at whose door she could lay the blame of her misfortune, and adopted a very hostile attitude towards Laura whenever their paths crossed. Up until now, Laura had managed to find some good excuse for her absence during her father's country gatherings which inevitably included Caroline Carmichael, for Sir George and her late husband had been close friends for years, and being a kindly man Sir George had not had the heart to exclude her from these gatherings, even though her presence was now more of an embarrassment than a pleasure, particularly as he had taken the cure. With the rose-tinted spectacles off, he continually blessed his good fortune in escaping the clutches of a thoroughly tiresome woman.

Rebecca's thoughts roamed on as she heard the

low murmur of voices in the background of her reverie. From what she could hear, Sir George was escorting several of his guests on a tour of the gardens, and from her recumbent position she caught sight of John dutifully following the small party and escorting Mrs Layman, a prominent member of the Cabinet, on the tour.

Her gaze turned to one of amusement as she watched him stoop to retrieve the lady's hat that had been dislodged from its precarious position on top of an enormous bun of hair by a sudden breeze, and her smile widened to a grin as she saw the hat take off again only a few yards further down the garden path, and was again retrieved by John.

Dear John, she thought, as the strolling figures passed out of sight. Why couldn't she accept his love and devotion? It would be so safe and sensible to fall in love with him, in spite of what Laura had said about the family smothering her, and how her life would be moulded around the political scene, but Rebecca had the inward assurance a woman has when she is certain of the extent of her husband's love for her, and that she would be the first consideration where John was concerned.

His behaviour towards her during her stay had proved that he was a man of his word, and he had made no outward onslaught on her, but contented himself with sending her intensive looks that spoke of his undying affection for her. She drew in her breath sharply. It was no use pretending that she could ever feel anything more for him than friendship. That she would ever feel anything for any man, come to that, she thought shrewdly, and frowned at the thought. Perhaps something had been left out of her make-up. She had never suffered the pangs of first love, and indeed never wanted to. Love, as she saw it, was something she could do without, but friendship was different. She had lots of friends, but she was still free, and that was how she intended to keep things.

She was not alone in this outlook. There was Barbara, who was a few years older than Rebecca, although in Barbara's case she had been in love, and was still in love as far as Rebecca knew, but had been unfortunate enough to settle her affections on a charming rogue who had sponged on her good nature financially until he had snared a richer prize and promptly married a wealthy widow.

To Rebecca's way of thinking, Barbara should have considered herself well rid of such a man, but she knew with certainty that given the opportunity Barbara would have welcomed him back with open arms. She shook her head sadly. Such was the idiocy of love.

Rebecca's mind went over the men she had met, and that she had only to give some encouragement to, to receive a proposal of marriage from. She was not stupid enough not to realise that her looks had attracted more than the usual attention from the male fraternity. Nature had been most generous in regard to her physical features, and this had proved a handicap in her career.

She was not expected to have a career, that was plain enough, and it had taken a long time for the message to get through to even the most studious members of the College that she loved her work and had no plans to seek a husband to support her at the earliest given opportunity.

Endowed as she was with more than her share of what was considered beauty, she had had ample opportunity of observing the frailties of human nature, particularly where it concerned the opposite sex, and where age was no barrier. She had seen older men, who should have had more sense, make fools of themselves when out of the eagle eye of their spouses, and all supposedly pillars of respectability. As for their younger counterparts— Rebecca sighed. It was hardly surprising that she had a jaundiced view of the marital state, or of the male sex as a whole.

There were exceptions, of course. Old Professor Dawson, for instance, was a pet, and she was quite fond of the Bursar, both of whom lived solely for their work, but they were the only two in the whole College that she could feel entirely at ease with and not have to watch points with, or find herself having to adopt an air of icy reserve against a sudden gleam of speculation she would spot in a predatory male's eyes while she went about her secretarial duties.

Rebecca turned over on to her back. She ought to have got a job in a bank, or an accountants' office, she thought dryly, tucked away in some dreary office with a boss whose sole target was aimed at making more money. Or with that detestable author, who was only concerned with his precious work, and didn't care who typed it, as long as they were competent. She could have been a

robot for all the notice he had taken of her, she
thought indignantly, and felt a spurt of pleasure at
having walked out on him. She was not used to
that kind of treatment, although she had to admit
that she preferred that approach to the apologetic,
slavish one she had often encountered in the past.

She gave a grin. You certainly knew where you
stood with a man like that, and it was a pity that
he couldn't have been a bit more likeable in his
manner, but she supposed fame had gone to his
head. With success in the literary field, and
undoubted success in the petticoat stakes, judging
by the amount of calls he had received from husky-
voiced charmers while Rebecca was in his employment, she couldn't see how he could avoid becoming self-opinionated, it was a natural sequence, and
just scored another point in her soured outlook as
far as men were concerned.

'Is this another cure for the mumps?' asked a
voice somewhere above Rebecca that made her
wonder if she was having an hallucination, for it
was the voice of the man she had just been thinking
about.

As if doubting the evidence of her ears she sat
up straight, and her startled eyes met Janus Leon's
impersonal stare. How on earth, she thought, did
he come to be at Pinehurst, and what had Barbara
let her in for?

'You've made a remarkable recovery, I see,' he
went on sarcastically. 'False alarm, was it?' he
asked with a sceptical glint in his eyes.

For the want of a better reply, Rebecca said,
'Er—yes.' There was nothing else she could say,

she thought, but she promised herself a few words with Barbara at the earliest opportunity.

'Working for Sir George, are you?' Janus Leon asked conversationally, as he dropped down beside her lounger. 'I guess English titles have a lot of sway here,' he added meaningly. 'Got yourself a nice little number, by the look of things,' he added significantly, his knowing eyes flicking over her skimpy sunsuit.

Rebecca wished she had something she could cover herself up with, and resented not only his tone but his cool appraisal of her figure. 'How did you know I was here?' she asked, more for something to say than real curiosity, although she could guess where his information had come from, he must have bullied Barbara for it.

Janus Leon subjected her to a long cool stare. 'Don't flatter yourself,' he drawled. 'I didn't know.' His glance rested on her hair. 'If you wish to remain incognito you should do something about that hair of yours. It's like a beacon to interested parties,' he added with a grin that had all the trimmings of a wolf on the prowl, and Rebecca recognised the signs, and for some unaccountable reason felt he had let her down; he was just another hunter out for a scalp.

'I'm not trying to hide myself!' she retorted indignantly. 'I happen to be one of Sir George's guests,' she added coldly, meaning to put this cocksure man in his place.

Janus Leon's eyes narrowed as he gazed ahead of him. 'He's a widower, isn't he?' he said dryly, leaving Rebecca to draw her own conclusions on this comment, which she did, and wanted to slap his face for the suggestion that she was there for one purpose only.

'He also happens to be the father of a good friend of mine,' Rebecca got out icily, and stood up quickly. 'You'll find Sir George down on the lower terraces,' she added firmly, showing him that she had better things to do than to stay bandying words with him.

'What's the hurry?' he drawled, reaching up with a deceptively casual hand towards her, and as she moved to avoid contact with him, caught her hand with a swift almost catlike sureness, forcing her to stay beside him until he chose to release her.

'Would you mind letting me go?' she asked politely. She had been in too many similar situations in the past to lose her temper. She had seen it all before.

'As I said,' he remarked coolly, 'what's the hurry? So we're both guests. I know your name and you know mine, and there's no reason why we shouldn't get better acquainted with each other, is there? You know,' he went on smoothly, 'I'm a great believer in fate. Sure, I was riled when you skipped out on me like that. You're good at your job, I'll say that for you,' his blue stare once again subjected her to a cool appraisal. 'You're also easy on the eye. It's not often one finds that combination. Okay, I take back what I said just now. You're here on the level as a friend of the family. I'm here as an acquaintance of Sir George, and for an English background for a novel I've had in mind for some time. I gather,' he went on dryly, 'that there won't be too many young things around on this party. Sir George was worried that I might find things a bit dull from that angle. However,' he shot her a sidelong glance, 'that was before I found you, and so far I've no complaints,' he added meaningly.

Rebecca took the opportunity of removing her hand from his grasp before she answered this cool assumption of his that she would be willing to lighten his stay at Pinehurst by indulging in a light flirtation with him. His look and his remarks were too pointed for her to misinterpret his meaning. 'I shall be pleased to do anything I can to help you get the background for the novel,' she said quietly, 'and I'm sure John will too,' she added meaningly.

'John?' queried Janus Leon with a raise of the eyebrows.

Rebecca nodded graciously. 'Sir George's son,' she supplied a little maliciously, taking pleasure in the narrowing of his very blue eyes as he worked out the implication of this news.

'Your friend?' he asked in a silky voice. 'Well, well!'

Rebecca flushed as she caught the sarcasm in his voice, but replied readily enough, 'Yes,' and glancing towards the gardens, remarked, 'Oh, here's Sir George now. I'll go and change for lunch while I've got the opportunity,' and she walked off towards the house, conscious the whole time of those hard blue eyes boring into her back.

Before lunch, as was the custom, everybody assembled in the green drawing room adjoining the dining room, and Rebecca, who had told Laura of the arrival of the novelist, but nothing else, stood beside John and Laura and watched the introductions being carried out to the few guests who had not as yet met the author.

His arrival had caused quite a stir even among these dedicated politicians, who, it appeared, had all heard of him, even if they were not avid readers of his books, and Rebecca was reminded of a remark of Barbara's on her enforced confinement in the College, and how she knew little of the world outside the cloisters of the College, and she had to admit ruefully to the truth of this statement.

While she sipped her sherry and made desultory remarks to Laura and John, her bemused eyes watched Janus Leon receiving accolades from several of the guests who had clustered round him. That he was used to this kind of reception was obvious from the way that he handled the interested questioning about his work.

When Mrs Carmichael pushed herself forward, exclaiming how much she had enjoyed his last novel, and proceeded to hog his attention, Laura gave Rebecca a knowing nudge of the elbow, and they both watched with amused interest as she determinedly cut across other questions in her bid to capture his attention.

'I must admit,' murmured Laura, 'that he's a gorgeous hunk of man. He's got brains, too,' she added in a half-surprised voice. 'Did you read *Devil's Ploy*?' she asked Rebecca. 'If you haven't, you must. It's fabulous! They say there's talk of making it into a film. Oh, I do wish that wretched woman would come away and give someone else a chance to talk to him,' she added crossly.

Rebecca gave her an amused glance. 'Don't worry,' she said teasingly, 'he's here for the week, remember? You'll get your chance later.'

Laura pulled a face at this. 'Want to bet?' she asked dryly. 'She'll latch on to him like a leech. Give Daddy some peace, I suppose,' she added thoughtfully, 'although she's not entirely given up hope in that direction yet,' she tacked on meaningly.

Sir George was apparently of the same mind as his daughter where Mrs Carmichael's monopolisation of the author was concerned, and with a skilful manoeuvre worthy of his political status managed to tear him away and continue with the introductions.

'This is Colonel Franly,' he said, introducing a stout rather bucolic-looking man, whose mild voice did not match his looks. 'Just back from the Middle East. He could tell you a thing or two on the latest machinations out there—eh, Franly?' and at the raising of Colonel's sandy eyebrows at this assertion, added jovially, 'well, what's printable!'

A few minutes later Rebecca was the next in line, and not knowing of her connection with Janus Leon, Sir George affected an introduction. On Janus Leon's nod of acknowledgment, and his quick, 'I'm acquainted with Miss Lindsey,' Rebecca received a jab in the side from the indignant Laura, who would no doubt take her up on that later, then it was Laura's turn to be introduced, since John had met their famous guest before the lunch assembly.

This completed the introductions, and with some annoyance Rebecca found that Janus Leon was in no hurry to move on and circulate, but elected to remain with their small group, although he could have attached himself to any of the other guests who were plainly longing to talk to him.

'I didn't know that you knew Rebecca,' said John, as the luncheon gong rang, and they all converged on the dining room.

'Oh, we met in the line of duty,' Janus Leon replied breezily. 'She was kind enough to type some of my novel for me.'

There was a smothered gasp from Laura at this, and Rebecca held herself in readiness for another dig in the ribs from her as she replied lightly for John's benefit, 'Barbara was in a hole, and I just helped out.'

She felt rather than saw Janus Leon's sharp glance at her as they arrived at the table, and to her further annoyance she found that she had been placed next to the wretched man with John on her left, and Laura practically opposite her on the other side of the table, and something told her that she was not going to enjoy this meal one little bit.

There was no shortage of conversation, for which Rebecca was grateful, and for once it did not centre around politics but on Janus Leon's novels, and she began to think she might enjoy her lunch after all.

A short while after this hope had been conceived, she found she had been a little previous in her optimism, for when a lull appeared in the conversation, and Sir George held the stage for a brief period, Rebecca found herself the subject of Janus Leon's attention. 'Doesn't he know you're a working girl?' he asked her in a low voice, audible only to her.

At first she could not get the connection, and when she did, she was furious. He was hinting that she had somehow wormed herself into high society for somewhat obvious reasons. 'Of course he does!' she replied, keeping her voice just as low as his, and then turned her attention back again to John who was asking her if she cared for a game of tennis after lunch.

'What were you two whispering about?' Laura demanded later after lunch, and the girls were on their way to their rooms to change for tennis.

'We weren't whispering,' Rebecca replied tetchily, for she was still smarting under Janus Leon's insinuations.

'Well, I couldn't hear what was said,' Laura replied pettishly. 'You're not having an affair with him, are you?' she asked curiously.

Rebecca threw her a look of high indignation. 'Certainly not!' she exclaimed in a voice that spoke of her feelings in no uncertain way.

Laura giggled. 'Well, I couldn't see it, somehow,' she said, as they reached their rooms, and instead of going into her room that was next to Rebecca's, followed her into her room. 'Well, what's the big secret, or aren't you going to tell me? You could have knocked me down with a feather when he said you'd met. Why didn't you tell me?'

Rebecca gave her an exasperated look. She wouldn't give up until she had heard the whole story, so she might as well get it over with, she thought, and launched into the story, ending with, 'As for telling you, I didn't know he was invited here for the weekend, did I? He was only a passing acquaintance anyway. I might have mentioned it had his name cropped up in the conversation,' she gave a light shrug, 'otherwise I wouldn't have given it a thought.'

Laura gave her a look that showed a certain amount of scepticism, and then sighed. 'All right, I believe you, thousands wouldn't, but I'll give you the benefit of the doubt only because I know you. I suppose working with all those learned men makes you a bit blasé.' She put her head on one side and gave Rebecca a considering look. 'What did he say to you?' she asked. 'Whatever it was, it annoyed you, I saw that much,' she added, then her eyebrows shot up. 'I say, did he make a pass at you?' she asked hopefully. 'I hear he's a bit of a playboy as far as the women are concerned.'

Rebecca drew in an exasperated sigh. She saw no reason for not telling the truth. 'He seemed to think I'd gatecrashed into high society,' she said dryly. 'Of course he'd got it in for me because I'd walked out on him,' she added. 'I only promised Barbara a week, but I couldn't tell him that. Barbara needs his monetary support,' she gave a smile. 'Apparently she told him I'd got mumps.'

Laura gave a hoot of laughter. 'Barbara was never good at covering up, but I should have thought she could have done better than that,' she said, and gave Rebecca a considering look. 'No wonder he's put out! I shouldn't imagine a thing

like that has ever happened to him before, not
where females are concerned anyway,' she added
in amusement.

The following week proved a very trying time
for Rebecca and not anything like the peaceful time
she had promised herself. Janus Leon seemed
determined to haunt her and attached himself to
her small set, which comprised the younger members of the party. In a way this was understandable,
but there were many occasions when he could have
taken himself off on other pursuits, particularly as
he was ostensibly there to gather material for a
novel, but Rebecca was convinced he was out to
cause her as much discomfort as possible, and suc-
ceeded, only she was determined not to let him see
that he had ruined the first week of her holiday.

To say that he shamelessly presumed upon their
slight acquaintance was putting it mildly. Rebecca
tried everything she knew to rebuff his attentions,
but apart from actually telling him that she wished
him elsewhere, cold looks and equally cold replies
to his bantering conversation made not the slightest
effect on him.

After four days of the chase, Rebecca's temper
was anything but sweet, and Laura's amused comment that Janus Leon must fancy her did nothing
to soothe her ruffled feelings, for the truth of the
matter was that he was out to annoy her. He hadn't
liked being given a set-down. He was used to idol-
atry, and Rebecca had broken a golden rule by not
joining the queue of his admirers.

Be it tennis, or swimming in the luxurious pool
at the back of the house, Rebecca could always be

sure of company—John on one side of her, and the big game hunter on the other side. She had ceased to think of him as an author, famous or otherwise, he was just another persistent male she had got stuck with, and one who was proving as stubborn in his attentions as she was to repel them.

It went without saying that she was fervently looking forward to the end of the week when she would be able to continue her holiday without the annoying presence of one egotistical male. As she had expected, she had been asked to stay as long as she wished, and it was only the thought of the peace to come that kept her from inventing some excuse to leave the house party early.

Rebecca was not the only one looking forward to the end of the week. John was showing signs of restiveness, like a volcano about to explode. As Janus Leon was one of his father's guests he could hardly order him off the premises, although he would have dearly loved to. The only saving factor that kept matters on a low key was the fact that Rebecca had not encouraged the attentions she was receiving from the author.

As Janus Leon was Rebecca's bugbear, Mrs Carmichael was Laura's. She had attached herself to the younger set for obvious reasons, and made an uncomfortable fifth at tennis, which meant that someone had to drop out after each game to accommodate her, and what made it worse was that she was a very mediocre player and promptly ruined any chance of a good set, for the others were all good players.

Relations between Laura and Caroline Carmichael only just stopped short of open warfare. Out of Sir George's proximity, the gloves were off as far as Caroline Carmichael was concerned, and she never failed to grasp an opportunity to belittle Laura.

Laura, however, was made of sterner stuff, and usually gave as good as she got. It was a game of very polite backhanders. So far the score was even, but it hardly helped to make the atmosphere a carefree one.

Where Rebecca was concerned, she welcomed the older woman's presence. Caroline was not one to stand aside and let others take the stage, not the female of the species anyway, and it did give Rebecca some leeway where Janus Leon was concerned, and though she could sympathise with Laura, her instinct for self-preservation took precedence!

The row that had been simmering between Caroline Carmichael and Laura finally broke during dinner on the Thursday evening.

The conversation had centred on the evening's entertainment when Sir George had suggested that the young folk might like to amuse themselves by dancing to the radiogram in the loggia off the conservatory, instead of taking part in the bridge sets usually made up among the guests.

This suggestion was met with consternation from Rebecca, who had dreaded such an event. So far she had managed to keep within a comfortable distance from Janus Leon, and had got used to the mocking challenge in his vivid blue eyes whenever their glances met. It was this look of his that had made her determined to keep her distance. It said all that she had suspected about him—that he was playing with her, and she was absolutely certain that should she attempt any concession in her attitude towards him, she would meet with the kind of set-down she had handed out to him, but for entirely different reasons. His was the evening up of a score, while hers was the simple fact that she did not care for the man.

To Rebecca's relief Laura, for reasons of her own, not least the thought of spending the whole evening in the detestable Caroline Carmichael's company, for it went without saying which of the entertainments she would choose, since she was as accomplished at bridge as she was at tennis and sorely tried whoever her unfortunate partner turned out to be, vetoed the suggestion with a firm, 'I'd rather read a book. How about you, Rebecca?' she asked, giving her a look that pleaded for her co-operation.

'Same here,' Rebecca replied quickly, not needing any encouragement to support Laura.

'I think a little dancing would be a splendid idea,' Mrs Carmichael cut in firmly, giving Laura a glare. 'You can read a book any time. The trouble is,' she said, turning confidingly to Sir George, 'these young people get too much leisure these days. My Joanna's a secretary in the Admiralty. No loafing about for her,' she tacked on spitefully, looking at Laura.

Under the table Rebecca's foot nudged Laura's in an effort to calm her down, but the danger signals were already there. Unwittingly, Caroline had touched upon one of Caroline's pet grudges against her father. She could do charity work, but no daughter of his was going out to work, etc, etc; and as Laura had no particular bent towards supporting old ladies behind the counter of a charity shop, or rushing about London in the dead of night with urns of soup for the down-and-outs, she remained a lady of leisure until she could get her father to take a more reasonable view of things.

'Aren't you a little tired, too?' Laura enquired of her arch-enemy, in a sugary sweet voice that made Caroline blink in surprise. 'I mean, tennis this morning, and a swim this afternoon—all that exercise! I know I'm tired, and so is Rebecca. Goodness knows how you keep up with us. I only hope I have half your energies when I get to your age.'

There was a moment's stunned silence after this sweet-sounding double-edged comment, and then everybody started talking at once. Sir George coughed, and Rebecca could not be sure if it was embarrassment or the effort of trying to keep his face straight that had brought on the coughing fit.

Mrs Layman, who intensely disliked Mrs Carmichael, and who looked as if she wanted to pat Laura on the back, declared heartily, 'Give me a good book any day, or a good game of bridge,' her pale blue eyes resting for a moment on Caroline Carmichael's outraged features as she struggled to compose herself.

There was no further mention of dancing, and as soon as Sir George settled down to a game of bridge with Mrs Layman and Colonel Franly,

Rebecca accepted John's invitation for a walk in the garden, and did not miss the narrowing of Janus Leon's eyes at her quick acceptance of the suggestion. It was an invitation she had refused the previous evening from Janus on an excuse of tiredness.

The evenings had been even worse for her than the days, as she did not play bridge, neither did Laura, and if she had hoped for a quiet evening's chat with Laura, Janus Leon had soon disabused her of that hope, for he elected to join the abstainers, solely on account of Rebecca's abstinence, she was sure, and to give him another chance of annoying her.

John had no such excuse, and as the guests were now down to a mere four—five if one counted Rebecca, he was needed to make up a set. Caroline Carmichael was under no such obligation, and promptly joined the abstainers, not wanting to miss a chance of getting Janus Leon to herself.

That, however, was how it had been the previous evening, but with Mrs Carmichael flouncing off to bed declaring that she had a headache, and throwing Laura a look that plainly said who had caused it, the evening, from Laura's point of view anyway, looked a more promising prospect.

The walk in the garden was not a very good idea, Rebecca soon found, for as she had suspected, John proposed to her, but as it had been a case of any port in a storm, she could not very well complain, and she managed to steer the conversation on to other channels after a gentle refusal, wishing once again that she did feel something for him, because she had been plagued with a restless feeling lately that was foreign to her nature and she could only put it down to dissatisfaction with everything in general.

Her gaze rested on a particularly lovely white rose climber on the trellis ahead of them. What was the matter with her? Why should she feel so dissatisfied with everything? She had a good job, hadn't she? Not a very exciting one, it was true, but who wanted excitement? Her fingers caressed the white silk petals of the roses when they reached the trellis, one half of her listening to John telling her how much he was looking forward to a week of peace on Saturday when the guests would have gone, and something about not giving up hope of her finally accepting him, the other half trying to come to terms with whatever ailed her.

Excitement, she thought—was that what was wrong with her? Had the short spell of work that she had done for Janus Leon aroused these thoughts? She had admittedly enjoyed the work, particularly as he had abided by her wish to leave her to get on with the work and had kept out of her way, and what a difference that had been from the role he was now adopting!

She sighed inwardly. She was tired of college work, she might as well admit it. She had caught a glimpse of other more interesting occupations and it had unsettled her. Perhaps she ought to join Barbara, she thought dryly. With the redoubtable Margaret keeping Janus Leon quiet, she could take on other assignments.

Her hand dropped suddenly away from the rose

as she envisaged herself seated at one of the desks
in the bureau office. No, that was not for her. At
least in the College she could move around. She
gave another inward sigh. She was just being
stupid. When she got back to work she would
wonder how she had ever imagined herself doing
other work, she fevently hoped that this would be
so; if not, she would have to look for other work,
only she had no idea what.

The following morning, Rebecca found herself
accompanying Janus Leon on a tour of the gardens. It had all been arranged so adroitly that she
had had no chance of getting out of it.

It appeared her offer of assisting him in collecting data for his novel had proved a rash one,
for he had taken her up on it, choosing a time
when John was otherwise engaged, being delegated
the task of going down to the local station to collect
a unique species of orchid for his father, whose
hobby was growing these exotic plants.

As soon as breakfast was over, Janus Leon presented her with a notebook, and remarked casually
that he was accepting her kind offer of assistance
in collecting background data for his novel.

It took Rebecca a moment or two to work out
what he was talking about, and seeing her look of
bewilderment, he said with a grin, 'You can take
notes for me on the background scenery.'

Hearing this, Laura said eagerly, 'Oh, I'm the
one to help you there. There's lots of history about
the place Rebecca wouldn't know about.'

Not to be outdone, Mrs Carmichael also offered
her services. 'My memory goes back a lot further

than yours. It must be accurate, you know,' she added maliciously as she stared at Laura.

Whatever Laura would have replied to this, and it would have been something on the lines of her last shot in their skirmish the previous evening at dinner, was fortunately defused by Janus Leon's smooth query as to whether either of them could take dictation, which settled the matter, and he waved aside any further offers of assistance by remarking, 'It's just my own impressions I'm after. I'm not looking for historical data,' and swept Rebecca off before Sir George, who had just joined them, added his offer of accompaniment.

The morning was a bright sunny one, in contrast to an overclouded one the previous day, and Rebecca thought about the coming week, and hoped the weather would be as kind as it had been that week. In fact, she concentrated on anything but the fact that she had been railroaded into spending a morning alone with the man she had gone to great pains to keep at a respectable distance. Under the circumstances, she could not have refused; in any case he had taken care that she had no chance of refusing.

By now they had reached the trellis walk that she had walked with John the previous evening, and she was reminded of her thoughts and how unsettled she had felt, and told herself it was all the fault of this wretched man. If he hadn't been such a hard taskmaster she wouldn't have had to help Barbara out and would have never experienced other work that had made her dissatisfied with her own job.

'You seem a bit tetchy this morning,' Janus remarked, as they left the trellised walk and walked on towards an ornamental pool that looked clear and refreshing in the morning sunlight. 'Didn't he come up to scratch?' he asked, as he stood surveying the scene in front of him through narrowed eyes.

Rebecca, who had opened the notebook ready to take notes as soon as he had stopped, glared at him. 'Do you want me to take notes, or are you going to turn this into an inquisition?' she demanded angrily.

Janus looked back at her standing a little behind him, and for a moment she caught a blaze of fury in his blue eyes; the next moment he was back to the mocking stage. 'So he did propose, but it wasn't what you were angling for,' he said dryly. 'I thought he looked a bit down when you came back.'

Rebecca's small sandalled foot tapped out her annoyance and impatience with this maddening man, and she kept her eyes on the notepad and the pen held in readiness.

He seemed to be in no hurry to oblige her. 'You know, looks aren't everything,' he said smoothly, 'and not in this class. It's background that counts. Now if you were Lady Peabody's daughter—well, that would be different. The chap's crazy about you, okay, but he'll have to watch his P's and Q's when it comes to matrimony.'

He moved on past the pool and towards the open parkland section, and Rebecca, after quelling an urge to turn her back on him and go back to the house, slowly followed him. She might as well let him enjoy himself, she thought, and regretted the fact that she had had to turn John down, if only to make this detestable man rearrange his thinking.

To her amazement, Janus suddenly lost interest in her relationship with John and started to give dictation. His portrayal of the woodland scene in front of them surprised Rebecca with its accuracy, correctly identifying the species of trees, and mentioning many details that she would have missed had she tried to describe it.

His botanical knowledge particularly surprised her, and forgetting their differences, she asked, 'Have you studied this?'

He turned from his surveillance of the scene and looked at her. 'Because I'm an Australian, you mean?' he replied. 'I went to university here. Cambridge, as a matter of fact.' His bright blue gaze flicked over her slight figure briefly as he added, 'We didn't have a glamorous bursar's secretary then, but it was a bit before your time, wasn't it?'

Rebecca's eyes returned to the notebook. Blast Laura! she thought crossly. He had evidently not wasted much time in pumping her for information about her.

'A bit dull, I should think,' he went on casually. 'All those learned men, but some of the dons are younger, aren't they? That's where you met John Sanderson, of course. Still, as I said, there's no future in that direction. Not according to his sister, and she ought to know.'

Rebecca stared down at the notes she had made,

but her hand that held the book trembled slightly with rage. Of all the detestable men! What right had he to discuss her with Laura, or anyone else come to that? Quite apart from the fact that he had put the wrong interpretation on Laura's assertion that she would never marry John. As clever as he was, he did not know the half of it.

For the next thirty minutes Rebecca followed him round the estate taking copious notes, and having got all that he required in the form of material he suggested that they take a breather, and indicated a garden seat opposite the garden pool.

So far Rebecca who had managed to contain her temper, adopting a businesslike attitude and refusing to reply to his earlier personal remarks, now wondered if he was going to make a pass at her. Considering that he thought her a scheming woman out to better herself by marrying into the aristocracy, he would consider her fair game.

Oddly enough, she was not alarmed, even though they were some way away from the house, and if he had some such plan in mind, she could expect no help.

He watched her eyes as they lingered on the seat, then went back to him, and correctly interpreted her thoughts. 'I'm not going to get amorous,' he said dryly. 'I've got a business proposition to put to you.'

Rebecca's lovely deep blue eyes widened in surprise. What an extraordinary man he was! she thought, as she settled down on the seat, taking care not to sit too near him, for she still did not trust him.

'Look, you're wasting your time here,' he said abruptly. 'I've been thinking about what you said about my needing a personal secretary, and you were right.' His eyes that had been surveying the pool now suddenly rested on her. 'I'm offering you the post,' he said.

Rebecca wanted to say yes, but something held her back. It was what she wanted, wasn't it? Why then had she to refuse him? Because she knew that she *was* going to refuse him. Her lovely eyes stared back at him. What was it about him that so annoyed her? Was it his arrogance, or was it her pride because he persisted in thinking the worst of her? She wasn't used to that kind of treatment. Either way, it wouldn't work. She took a deep breath. 'Thank you for the offer,' she said quietly, 'but I'm afraid I must refuse—I'm quite happy where I am,' she added firmly.

He hadn't liked that at all, she noticed, although she had given her reply without any trace of antagonism. 'Liar!' he said softly. 'You're not going to give up hope where Sanderson's concerned, are you? Fancy yourself as Lady Sanderson one day, do you?' He stood up abruptly. 'If there's anything I can't stand it's a snob,' he said harshly. 'That's where we Aussies can teach you Brits a lesson. We accept folk for what they are, not what they've got. As for titles, we don't bow and scrape over there.' He stared at the notebook in Rebecca's hand. 'Could I prevail upon your kindness to transcribe that?' he asked sarcastically. 'I've got a portable typewriter in my car.'

Rebecca was still smouldering over his unfair accusation that she was a snob. 'Any stenographer could do it,' she said coldly. 'My shorthand is perfectly legible,' and she thrust the book towards him.

He did not take it but stood looking at her through hooded lids. 'I'll pay for the work. Let's see, we've spent about an hour on this, haven't we? Whatever your price is I won't quibble. Do the transcribing and I'll double it,' he said harshly.

Two bright spots of colour adorned Rebecca's cheeks. It wasn't so much what he had said about giving her price, but the way he had said it, making her feel like a street walker. He'd meant to be insulting too, just because she had refused him. She stood up abruptly and put the notebook down on the seat with a firmness that surprised her, for she was absolutely furious and would have liked to throw it at him. Her eyes flashed sparks of fury as they clashed with his bright blue ones that flashed back an answering warning. 'You couldn't afford me, Mr Leon,' she said haughtily. 'I'll present you with my time for free!' and with her head held high, she marched off towards the house. If he dared to address her again, she would slap his face, she thought furiously, no matter who witnessed it!

CHAPTER FOUR

WHEN Rebecca reached the house, she went straight up to her room, glad that she had encountered neither Laura nor John, who were probably down by the swimming pool awaiting her arrival, but she was in no mood for social chat. She needed a little time to compose herself after her head-on clash with Janus Leon, not to mention his extraordinary offer. Why on earth had he to pick on her? As famous as he was, he would have no trouble in getting staff. Her soft lips firmed as the thought occurred to her that he had only been trying it on, just testing, as they say, and if she had said yes—Her smooth brow creased. He had meant it, of this she was certain. Whatever else he was, he was not the type of man to waste time on petty revenges.

She shook her head slowly. How on earth he had expected her to accept the job after accusing her of running after John for purely mercenary reasons was beyond her. She only hoped he showed more tact when interviewing the numerous applicants for the post when it was advertised.

Rebecca gave a light shrug at this thought. It was no concern of hers, happily. Anyone was welcome to the job, and she couldn't think of a more miserable position than to be in constant contact with a man like that.

Feeling much more cheerful, she changed out of her dress and put her swimming costume on. She ought to get a bit of sunbathing in before lunch, she thought, noting that the time was only a little after eleven.

As she picked up her towelling wrap and collected her sunglasses the thought occurred to her that she ought to write to Barbara. She would be intrigued to learn who Rebecca had run into, not to mention the difficult position she had unwittingly put her into, with her not so brilliant idea of giving her the mumps!

Her smile faded as another thought occurred to her. What would happen to Barbara's business if Janus Leon took his work away from the bureau? She had said that she was only existing on a shoestring until she moved into the new premises, and whose fault would it be if he did? Hers, of course, she thought, and gave an inward groan. How could she have been so stupid! All because she had not liked the wretched man and had not intended to put herself out in any way to oblige him.

A sense of guilt swept over her. She ought to warn Barbara of the possibility of her losing her valued client, that was the least she could do. She would have to tell her that she had been offered the job, but had turned it down, and the sooner she did this the better. Forewarned is forearmed, she told herself, throwing her sunglasses down on the bed and getting out her writing materials before settling down on the window seat to write the letter.

She got through the first page easily enough, explaining how she had got a shock on finding that Janus Leon was one of Sir George's guests, and chiding Barbara for not thinking up a better excuse to explain her absence. The next part was going to be the tricky part for Rebecca. Barbara was not going to take kindly to the news, particularly when she found out that the whole idea of Janus's getting a personal secretary had come from her, and decided to only mention the fact that she had been offered the job, and the likelihood of his taking his business away from the bureau.

As she was about to set this down on paper her eye caught the tall figure of the man she was writing about. Her teeth, that had been chewing the top of her pen, clamped hard on the Biro top as she watched him striding towards the house, and as she recalled her parting shot to him, her lips relaxed into a smile of satisfaction. She had been too incensed earlier to enjoy her moment of triumph, but now that she had calmed down, she could appreciate the way she had handled things. He had had it coming, she thought, and would now avoid her like the plague, and she couldn't have wished for a better state of affairs.

She was still watching that tall proud figure coming towards the house when another person appeared walking in his direction. It was Caroline Carmichael, and Rebecca guessed that she had been waiting for him to return. However, after a few words Janus strode on again, leaving Mrs Carmichael staring after him with what looked like a look of frustration on her made-up face. Whatever she had suggested to the author, a walk in the gardens, perhaps, had been met with an abrupt refusal that had surprised her.

Rebecca allowed herself another smile. He was obviously still put out, and she wondered hopefully if he would decide to end his visit to Pinehurst on some excuse or other.

When the lunch gong rang, Rebecca had finished her letter to Barbara. She had decided to pay her another visit before she joined the College in five weeks' time. Time enough to find out if Janus Leon had taken his work away from the bureau, and if so, she would help Barbara out by investing some of the money her father had left her in the business, enough to tide her over until things got easier.

With that off her conscience, Rebecca went down to lunch, meeting John in the hall. 'Those wretched plants hadn't arrived,' he said dourly. 'I shall have to go down and meet the two-forty now.' He looked at Rebecca. 'I was back by ten-thirty,' he added, giving her an accusing look. 'I hear you spent the morning with Leon taking notes for him.'

Seeing Janus and Laura approaching the hall, Rebecca walked quickly into the dining room before she answered, 'Well, I did offer to give him some assistance in that line. He wanted an English background for his next novel.'

'I thought he wrote only Australian stories,' John replied a trifle sulkily as he seated her at the lunch table.

As Sir George, and Janus and Laura, then joined them, Rebecca was prevented from replying to this. Colonel Franly and Mrs Layman had left that morning, so when Caroline drifted in, late as usual, this completed the party, and lunch was served.

The absence of the other guests seemed to emphasise the atmosphere between Janus and Rebecca, or so Rebecca thought, for Janus gave all his attention to his host, Sir George, in between fending off pertinent questions from Mrs

Carmichael, who it appeared had decided to forgive his rather cavalier treatment of her that morning.

The rest of the afternoon was spent in lazing by the pool, and Rebecca, who had not been looking forward to another afternoon in the company of Janus Leon, particularly as John would not be around, having to go once again to the station, found to her delight that Sir George had taken on the task of entertaining his guest by showing him some old letters that dated back to Cromwellian times, and a few other treasures connected with the old house and that he was immensely proud of. Next to his hobby of growing orchids, the historical past of his forebears came a close second, and Rebecca felt that she could safely relax without the worry of her arch-enemy joining her during the afternoon.

Laura, however, was not so lucky, as her father had determinedly shaken off Caroline's attempt to share this exclusive showing of the treasures on the grounds that she had seen them before, against which there was no argument, and a frustrated Caroline had been forced to retire to the swimming pool.

Rebecca, lying stretched out beside the pool, and feeling the warm rays of the sun on her slim body, idly listened to Laura and Caroline having yet another disagreement, this time over what Laura termed as Sir George's lack of entertainment for his guests, for she was still sulking over his acceptance of Laura's and Rebecca's plea of tiredness the evening before when he had suggested that they dance to the radiogram. 'House parties,' she said in her high-pitched voice, 'are not what they used to be. We always made sure that our guests were entertained,' she went on pettishly, and gave a loud sigh. 'But that was in my husband's time, and he used to leave all that to me.'

Laura ought to have let this go and let her get on with it, but the bare fact that Caroline knew full well what Sir George's house parties consisted of, and precisely what type of guests were invited, was a little too much for her. 'Why don't you do some entertaining of your own?' Laura asked her caustically, knowing that one of Caroline Carmichael's drawbacks was that she had a grasping nature, and was always pleading poverty, yet Laura knew that her husband had left her very well provided for and she had often felt sorry for her daughters, who had had to exist on a pittance of an allowance during term time.

'As if I could afford to,' Caroline replied stoically. 'I've two daughters to provide for, remember.'

'Oh, I thought you said Joanna had a job. That leaves only one now, surely?' Laura replied sweetly.

Rebecca ceased listening at this point. She had a few things on her mind about herself to think about. It concerned the job that Janus Leon had offered her. If it had been anyone else but that man, she would have jumped at it. She sighed inwardly. Why had things to be so awkward? She now knew for certain that her days at the College were numbered. She needed a more stimulating job that would bring her out of the stifling confines of the College cloisters.

In an odd way she felt as if someone had tapped her on the shoulder and told her to wake up and start to live. She shook her head bewilderedly. This was not like her at all. Such thoughts had never entered her head before and it left her feeling lost and vulnerable, when she had always felt sure of herself.

A splash quite near her brought her out of her reverie and she saw that Laura had entered the pool and called for her to join her. 'Come on in! You've lazed long enough,' she commanded.

'Did you hear what she said about my being incapable of landing a job?' Laura burst out furiously, as they went into the house a short time later. 'It's a good job she's off home tomorrow. She did try and wangle another week out of Daddy, but thank goodness he wasn't having any,' she added fervently. 'And all that stuff about being hard up! Did you see that diamond brooch she was sporting the other evening? The truth is, she's as mean as they come. She could have brought poor old Sue with her, you know, Daddy wouldn't have minded, and Sue would have loved to come, but not her! She wouldn't want anyone in the way, not when she was hoping to get Daddy in a compromising situation!'

'Laura!' Rebecca protested in a half-amused but shocked voice. 'Look, I know you don't like the woman, neither do I, but do be careful what you say, someone might overhear you.'

'I don't care if they do!' Laura replied stubbornly. 'Everybody knows what she's like. She's ruined this house party. I'm sure that's why Mr and Mrs Rotherson left on Wednesday. When your author wasn't around she started fluttering her eyelashes at Sandy Rotherson. He's an up-and-coming member of the House and there's been a rumour that he might be knighted in the Birthday Honours List. She's not only after a second husband, but a title to boot. Mrs Rotherson soon got her number, though, didn't she, and carted him off.'

Rebecca was still recovering from Laura's casual assumption that Janus Leon was connected with her. 'All right,' she said soothingly. 'So we don't like her—and he's not "my author", by the way,' she added firmly. 'I hardly know the man. Cheer up,' she consoled her friend cheerfully, 'by lunch tomorrow we'll have the place to ourselves.'

In spite of this optimistic outlook, Caroline Carmichael, it seemed, had just one more spanner to throw into the works, and at dinner that evening she suggested that as it was the last evening of the house party, they should end it with a small party that would include dancing.

Under the circumstances, Sir George could not very well refuse, and this time neither Laura nor Rebecca had a say in the matter.

'I'm going to have a headache,' declared Laura, with a grin, 'and retire to bed with a good book,' as they went to their rooms ostensibly to dress for the party, and she advised Rebecca to do the same.

Rebecca would dearly have loved to be able to follow this advice, but two headaches would be a bit too much to swallow from the rest of the company's point of view, and Laura had thought of it first. 'A fine friend you've turned out to be,' she said bitterly to Laura. 'I came here in response to a plea of yours, and what happens? You drop out when the going gets rough. How can I cope on my own?' she demanded.

'You'll have a marvellous time,' Laura said unrepentantly. 'Just imagine it—John and Janus fighting over you all evening!' she added with a wide grin. 'I'd take Janus if I were you,' she tacked on earnestly. 'Not that I think that you'll have much choice. That man's got a certain look in his eye when he looks your way.'

'I'm not "taking" anyone,' Rebecca replied firmly. 'And I'm not going to enjoy it one little bit, thanks to you. Look,' she said pleadingly, 'you like Janus, don't you? Well, your father will have to dance with Caroline, won't he, and that leaves Janus for you. I'll be dancing with John.'

'Not all the time you won't,' Laura replied just as firmly. 'As for Daddy, I'll tell you just what will happen. He'll dance just once with that wretched woman, and having done his duty, he'll disappear into the conservatory and spend the rest of the evening with his beloved orchids. I'm not spending another evening in that woman's company. I've taken all I'm going to take from her,' she added emphatically.

Rebecca knew when she was beaten and left her, and went into her room to get dressed.

The evening promised to be as delightful for Rebecca as Laura thought it would be for her, and what with John determined to put Janus Leon out, and Janus doing his utmost to annoy her, at this thought her hand stilled on the zip she was about to pull up on her evening dress, a light silky dress of a delicate blue with a floating skirt, but with a straight classical top. Surely after what had happened that morning, Janus would simply ignore her, wouldn't he? As he had more or less for the rest of that day, in which case John had nothing to worry about, she thought with a smile, and neither had she! It was a good thing, she thought comfortably, that Laura would not be there to witness Caroline finding herself the belle of the ball and receiving all of Janus Leon's attention, for that she could not have borne, she told herself, as she took one last critical look at herself before leaving her room.

She did not go straight down to join the others, but looked in on Laura first in the hope that she might have changed her mind, but one look at her sprawled across her bed with her head in a paperback immediately doused this hope. 'I'm off,' she said unnecessarily, trying to work up some enthusiasm for the evening in store.

Laura raised her head and stared at her. 'You look stunning,' she said. 'Are you sure you don't like Janus?' she asked with a twinkle in her eye.

Rebecca did not bother to answer and left the bedroom, almost colliding with Caroline as she was just passing Laura's room.

If Rebecca had disbelieved Laura's assertion that Caroline was not a poor woman, her dress that evening would have convinced her. Rebecca knew about clothes, and the evening dress she was wearing cost more than she would have been prepared to pay for such an item. It was a gossamy, floating creation in a shocking pink, designed for a much younger woman, Rebecca surmised, but worn by Caroline Carmichael with a determination to impress. Her scent, that wafted towards Rebecca, was a little strong for her taste, and like the dress was a recognisably expensive one.

As Rebecca was taking stock of Caroline's dress, so was Caroline pricing Rebecca's. 'Pretty,' she said. 'I go for more definite colours,' she added, and looked behind Rebecca. 'No Laura?' she asked hopefully.

Rebecca said something about Laura having a headache and Caroline smiled knowingly. 'I don't suppose she knows what to wear,' she said in her high-pitched voice. 'Not at all sociable. She must be a great trial to her father—but then her mother was the same,' she added, 'hardly helpful to Sir George's position, I always thought.'

Rebecca did not reply, and fervently hoped that Laura had not heard what Mrs Carmichael had said, although she suspected that that had been the whole point of the exercise.

When they reached the patio next to the conservatory that was being used as the dancing area, and was of ample proportions to accommodate such a small party, Sir George insisted on them visiting the conservatory to view his latest acquisition.

John, not unnaturally, was less enthusiastic than the others, considering that he had spent most of the day meeting various trains until the plant had eventually arrived, allowing him just about time to get back to dinner, declined the offer and set himself the task of selecting records for the evenings entertainment.

Only after duly admiring the purple orchid with its bright orange flecks were they allowed to return to the patio, and Rebecca for one was glad to escape out of the claustrophobic atmosphere of the conservatory, in spite of the perfumed blossoms around them, and get back into the fresher air, and judging by the way her example was followed by Caroline and Janus, they were of the same opinion. Sir George, who must have been a little disappointed at the briefness of their stay, joined them as the first record started to play.

Rebecca, who had been confidently looking forward to an evening of peace, where Janus Leon was concerned anyway, was dismayed to find that Caroline Carmichael was not the only one capable of forgoing a grudge where her own interests were concerned. Janus also had apparently chosen to ignore Rebecca's scornful rejection of his offer, and acted as if nothing had happened.

It might have been the thought of finding himself partnering Caroline throughout the evening that brought about this state of affairs, but whatever it was, Rebecca would have preferred things left as they were, and now she found herself having to dance first with John and then with Janus, with no respite, for Sir George, after partnering Caroline for the first dance, wandered, as Laura had predicted, back into the conservatory.

On the face of things, Rebecca ought to have enjoyed herself, but each time she danced with Janus she was acutely aware of him. Dressed in a dark tuxedo and crisp white shirt, he made a dynamic force to be reckoned with, and she could well understand his success with the opposite sex.

His attitude towards her caused her even more discomfort. If anything, he was over-polite, much as one treated a stranger, and his conversation was as far removed from the personally antagonistic attitude he had previously adopted towards her as was possible, and made Rebecca wonder if she had imagined their previous furious encounter, but she hadn't, and her eyes were wary whenever they met his bland ones.

Half-way through the evening, a diversion came, and one that was not unwelcome from Rebecca's point of view. Janus had annoyed John by holding Rebecca a little closer than was strictly necessary, and John, keeping a watching brief on any such action, not only took note, but took umbrage as well, and was barely civil when Janus spoke to him, and Rebecca, seeing heavy weather ahead, decided to sit out the next dance with Janus; it was safer than dancing with him. Only her persistency in keeping a reasonable distance from him while dancing had prevented him from adopting the more intimate style of dancing cheek to cheek with her.

It was at this convenient time that Caroline Carmichael returned from the cloakroom in an agitated state and announced that she had lost her diamond brooch, and demanded that an immediate search was held to find it, wailing, 'I ought to have got the clasp seen to!' as the search began.

When it was not found in the immediate vicinity, or in the downstairs cloakroom that Rebecca checked in case Caroline had missed it, Rebecca tried to remember whether she had seen Caroline wearing it that evening, in spite of her assertion that she had worn it, but glancing at the frothy neckline of Caroline's gown, she had to admit that she wouldn't have noticed it if she had worn it, the layers of frill would have hidden it.

By now, the staff had been brought into the search, and as no sign of the brooch was found, Sir George inclined towards Rebecca's theory that Caroline had not worn it that evening, and the search was extended to her bedroom and private bathroom, in spite of Caroline's furious denial that she had not left the brooch there.

Time went by, and no sign of the brooch was found, although the whole house had been searched, apart from the servants' quarters, and all the areas that Caroline would have visited during the day, for it was recalled that she had worn the brooch earlier in the day, and as things began to look serious, with Caroline making dark hints about the brooch having been stolen, Sir George was obliged to widen the search for his own satisfaction, if not Mrs Carmichael's, who vehemently asserted again that she had worn the brooch, and it was no use looking elsewhere for it.

As each search proved negative, so Caroline became more positive that someone must have taken it, and at Sir George's indignant denial that anyone, including the staff, would have done such a thing, she retorted angrily, 'Well, where is it? It's not as if it was a small brooch. If I'd dropped it somewhere it would have been found by now.'

Sir George shook his distinguished head. 'Perhaps someone did find it, and put it down somewhere to return to you later,' he said slowly.

'After all this searching?' Caroline said sarcastically. 'By now the whole house knows I've lost the brooch, and it hasn't been returned, has it?' she added meaningly.

There was one person who didn't know, Rebecca thought suddenly. Laura did not know, and it would be just like her to find the wretched thing and not bother to chase downstairs to return it to its owner, particularly as they were on such bad terms.

As if Rebecca's thoughts had transferred themselves to Caroline, she suddenly exclaimed, 'Laura!' and marched out of the room, closely followed by Rebecca who could see squalls ahead if Laura was the culprit. Caroline was out for blood and she would like nothing better than to make trouble for Laura.

When they reached Laura's room Caroline swept in without bothering to knock, and an indignant Laura, in the process of getting undressed ready for bed, stared hostilely at the woman who had so presumptuously invaded her privacy.

Before Laura could air her views upon this intrusion, Caroline spat out, 'Have you taken my brooch?' in a rude accusing manner that brought an immediate response from Laura.

'I have not taken your brooch,' she said furiously, 'and it's customary to knock before entering someone's bedroom!' she added, as she slipped on a dressing gown and looked pointedly towards the door.

Taking the hint, Caroline flounced out of the room, muttering in a low venomous voice that she would get the police in the next day, whether George liked it or not.

Rebecca's eyes met Laura's glowering ones. 'It would be her that had to lose something, wouldn't it?' she said with a wry grin. 'She insisted that she wore it tonight, but with all those frills at her neck I honestly couldn't remember seeing it.'

Laura grimaced, then straightened her back. 'She dropped it in the passage,' she said offhandedly.

Rebecca's eyes widened. 'You mean you *have* got it?' she asked incredulously.

Laura nodded, and gave a grin. 'Serves her right,' she said crossly. 'She can stew now until tomorrow. I heard what she said earlier about being sorry for Daddy. That was bad enough, but when she brings my mother into it——' she drew a deep breath. 'She was a better person than she'll ever be,' she added, and looked at Rebecca. 'Don't worry,' she said in a light voice, 'I haven't taken to collecting jewellery. I don't like the thing anyway, it's a little too ostentatious for my liking. I'll put it on her dressing table after she's gone down to breakfast tomorrow. I can't very well give it to her now, can I?' she added with a grin. 'If she'd just asked me if I'd found it instead of accusing me of taking it, I would have told her I'd got it.'

'You can't leave it on her dressing table,' Rebecca said slowly, sounding worried. 'Sir George insisted I went with her to her bedroom to look for it in case she hadn't worn it. She was furious with him, but she had to agree, especially after dropping a few hints about it being stolen. You'll have to come up with another idea, although what, I can't think. The whole place has been searched.'

'Oh, come on, Rebecca!' Laura said lightly. 'You sound as if it was serious! When she finds the wretched thing on her dressing table tomorrow, she'll realise it was a joke. She'll be only too glad to get the thing back and will leave it at that.'

Rebecca shook her head. 'It's not as easy as that,' she said quietly. 'The very fact that it's now been returned means that someone did take it, at least that's how she'll see it, particularly as she's muttering about bringing in the police. Don't you see? She'll think someone's got cold feet. That puts us all under suspicion, only what John, or Janus Leon, would want with a diamond brooch——' She left the rest unsaid, but Laura caught her meaning.

'You mean, she'll think you took it?' she demanded disbelievingly.

Rebecca shrugged. 'Well, she did ask you point blank, didn't she?' she said quietly, 'and that leaves me.'

Laura took a deep breath. 'Very well,' she sighed, pulling the belt of her dressing gown round her, 'I'll go and confess. I won't like it, in fact I shall hate it, but I'm not having you accused,' she added quietly.

Rebecca shook her head. 'I shouldn't do that either,' she said firmly. 'Not in the mood she's in at the moment. She's simply furious with your father for disbelieving her, and she's out for blood. If only you'd just said that you hadn't taken it but had found it,' she sighed, 'but it's too late now. I simply can't see her accepting your explanation without making trouble.'

Laura frowned. 'But I don't see how she can make trouble. Daddy will put a stop to anything like that, he'll believe me and not her, if she tries to accuse me of pinching it.'

There was silence for a moment, then Laura uttered a heartrending, 'Oh no!' that made Rebecca glance anxiously at her. 'I'm a first class fool,' she went on, and slapped her forehead with her palm. 'You know what I've done?' she asked Rebecca in a woebegone voice. 'I've just handed that woman what she's been angling for for months. I can see it now. In return for keeping quiet about poor Sir George's kleptomaniac daughter she'll expect a handsome reward, such as marriage—just to keep it in the family.' She shuddered. 'You're right,' she said dismally. 'I can't own up to it now. What on earth are we going to do, Rebecca?' she appealed wildly.

Rebecca was still getting over her friend's prediction of her father's fate. 'Surely she wouldn't——' she trailed off, as the fact presented itself that such a thing was highly probable.

'Oh, yes, she would!' declared Laura, cementing this thought.

Rebecca stared at her. 'Well, in that case, we

must think of somewhere to leave the brooch,' she said calmly, hoping to soothe Laura, who by now had her father already married to Caroline and all the misery such a state would bring in its train, 'and I shall have to do it.' She frowned. 'Thing is, where?' she said half to herself, then suddenly brightened. 'The conservatory!' she said happily. 'I'm certain a real search wasn't held in there.'

At Laura's puzzled look, she went on to explain how Sir George had prevailed upon them to visit the conservatory to admire his latest acquisition. 'We were only in there a short time,' she added, 'it was so uncomfortable in there, all that heat——' she gave a sigh of relief. 'That's where I'll leave it,' she decided. 'Put it somewhere near the orchid. It could easily have dropped off there. She said something about the clasp needing some attention.'

Laura gave her a weak grin. 'You'll earn my undying gratitude,' she said fervently, as she took the brooch out of the dressing table drawer and gave it to her.

CHAPTER FIVE

REBECCA was so busy with her thoughts, and so anxious to get rid of the brooch before meeting anyone with it in her possession, that she fairly hurtled down the corridor. Her idea had been a good one, she told herself, and all she wanted was a little luck in carrying it out. She would not even consider the possibility that Sir George might lock the conservatory at night—why should he? There were no orchid rustlers around, were there? Oh, dear, she thought, as she hurried along, she was getting slightly hysterical, and it was not at all funny.

By now she was downstairs, and blessing the fact that everybody seemed to have gone to bed, since there was only subdued lighting in the hall, and as she passed through it and into the passage leading to the dining room, and beyond that the lounge and library, through which she would have to pass, she hoped there would be some kind of lighting left on in the conservatory that would prevent her from blundering into any of the huge exotic arrangements of flowers that should she knock them down would be sure to awaken the whole household, but she decided to worry about that when she reached her goal. The main thing was to get there.

The crash came when she turned the bend in the corridor. She was going too fast to be able to avoid it, and her slight frame ran into what seemed to be an immovable object against which she collided full tilt and only managed to keep her balance by a steadying hand on her arm.

The brooch flew out of her hand on to the carpeted floor of the corridor, and her dismayed eyes followed its progress until it came to a scudding halt a yard or so down the corridor, and lay there seemingly leering at her as the bright facets of the jewels caught the dim corridor light.

It took her a shocked second or two to realise whose strong hand was steadying her and as she stared into two very blue eyes, her depression deepened. It would have to be him! she thought crossly, but managed to give him a bright smile, which was a mistake, considering that she had spent most of the week giving him the cold shoulder. 'Thank you,' she said breathlessly. 'I was rather hurrying—I wanted to get a book from the library before the lights were put out,' she explained quickly, hoping her explanation sounded plausible.

Janus Leon subjected her to a long look through narrowed eyes, then without saying a word walked back to where the brooch lay and picking it up, studied it for a second before turning back to Rebecca, whose legs began to feel decidedly wobbly as she watched him. If she had any sense she ought to have walked on past him, disclaiming any knowledge of the brooch's existence. He couldn't prove she had dropped it, she thought frantically.

'Going the wrong way, weren't you?' he said casually, glancing down at the brooch in his hand. 'Mrs Carmichael's room's on the second floor, isn't it?' he purred silkily.

Rebecca decided to stand her ground and declare that she didn't know what he was talking about, but something told her she was on a lost cause, but she had to try anyway. 'I came down to get a book,' she said coldly, and looked at the brooch in his hand. 'So you've found it,' she commented lightly. 'Sir George will be relieved. Mrs Carmichael too, of course,' she added, keeping her voice light despite the thudding of her heart.

'I saw it fly out of your hand at the collision,' he said in a smooth voice. 'What were you going to do with it? Leave it in the library until you could recover it?' he asked in a deceptively calm voice.

Rebecca took a deep breath. This was going to be difficult. Of all people to catch her with the wretched thing! Her lovely eyes met Janus Leon's hard gaze. 'You're not going to believe me,' she said quietly, 'but I was going to leave it in the conservatory to be found tomorrow. It wasn't taken by me—or anyone, if that's what you're suggesting. It was just an unfortunate oversight, that's all,' she added firmly.

Janus Leon's eyes said that he did not believe her, but when he spoke his voice was smooth—too smooth. 'I wish I could believe you,' he said, although Rebecca could detect no sympathy in his voice, only a kind of satisfaction, and the dreadful thought occurred to her that he was going to hand her over to Sir George to deal with, and if that happened, Laura would own up, and the fat would be in the fire.

'Do you make a habit of this sort of thing?' Janus went on in a hard voice. 'No wonder you can afford to dress well,' he added hatefully.

Rebecca wanted to slap his arrogant face. She also wanted to plead with him, to tell him the truth and explain how it was, and why it was so necessary that nothing was said. 'I did not take the brooch,' was all she said, not being able to come up with anything else. It was the truth after all, but again she knew he did not believe her.

At this point someone was heard approaching the corridor and Janus caught her arm in a steely hold in case she attempted to use the diversion as an escape, and as Stokes, the butler, walked towards them on his nightly locking-up rounds, Rebecca found herself swung into Janus's arms and being kissed in a way that no stranger ought to kiss a woman he hardly knew.

The impression of a spooning couple was well taken by Stokes, who murmured a polite 'Goodnight' to them as he passed. Being a good butler, he was neither surprised nor nonplussed, but treated the episode as a common occurrence that he was well familiar with, although Rebecca doubted if he had had occasion to witness such a scene before in Sir George's employment.

When the butler had gone, and before she could catch her breath, she found herself propelled into the small salon next to the library, and only freed from the iron hold Janus had on her when inside, and he had planted himself in front of the door to prevent her leaving.

Her lovely sapphire blue eyes flashed sparks of fury as she stared at the man who had dared to assault her like that. She felt she had been treated like a wanton—someone he had picked up and was amusing himself with. 'How dare you!' she got out in a low furious voice. 'Stand away from that door!' she commanded in a regal voice. 'I've told you the truth, and if you don't believe me it's just too bad. Do what you like with the wretched thing. Take it to Sir George!' she added, her temper making her tremble. 'I don't care. I've nothing to worry about.

You try anything like that on me again and I'll sue you for assault!' she spat out at him.

His piercing blue eyes narrowed to slits as he studied her, taking in her furious eyes and flushed cheeks, then he walked deliberately towards her and she backed slowly away from him. 'I mean it!' she said. 'Come any nearer and I'll scream the place down,' she threatened.

'I doubt if anyone would hear you if you did,' he said softly, still advancing. 'I know one sure way of stopping you if you do.'

Rebecca's small hands clenched on to the small occasional table against the wall. She could not move farther away, she was trapped. She knew she ought to feel panic-stricken, but she was too furious to feel any other emotion.

'Quite a little firebrand, aren't you?' Janus drawled silkily, now standing too near her for comfort, but her eyes did not flinch as they met his. 'We're going to have a little talk,' he went on, in a hateful smooth voice that Rebecca began to recognise and dislike heartily. 'It's up to you whether we reach a suitable conclusion—to our mutual benefit, I mean,' he added significantly.

Rebecca could see only one 'suitable conclusion' where he was concerned. She knew he had a reputation as a playboy, she also knew that she was not unattractive to the opposite sex. He must be enjoying this, she thought scathingly, there couldn't be many women who had given him the cold shoulder. Now she was going to pay for it. 'I'm not interested,' she snapped. 'You're wasting your time.'

His autocratic brows shot up at this, then he smiled at her, and Rebecca did not care for that smile at all, it had all the savour of a wolf just before the kill, and she began to feel the first pangs of fear. 'Don't be a fool,' Janus said harshly as her wide eyes showed her feelings. 'I don't suppose this is your first offence. You've been lucky before, haven't you? Or maybe you've managed to talk your way out of it—I suppose that's what you've got in mind now, isn't it? John Sanderson's crazy enough about you to cover things up, isn't he? But I'm a different proposition.'

He touched the slender strap of her evening gown. 'Very profitable too, wasn't it?' he said suggestively. 'I've heard of women like you. You ingratiate yourself with the wealthy.' He flicked a strand of her glorious hair with a careless finger. 'You've the looks to carry it off, too. If Sanderson had proposed, I guess you'd have behaved yourself, but things didn't work out, did they, and you couldn't resist making some profit out of a wasted week.' He gave another smile, but with no humour in it.

Rebecca said nothing, but her eyes spoke volumes. He was amusing himself at her expense, and when he had had enough he would hand her over to the authorities and somehow she would have to explain how she had come by the brooch without involving Laura. She drew in a deep breath. Let him go ahead with his accusations. No one would believe him. The College would give her a good reference, and there was John—she caught her breath as the thought occurred to her that that would put John in the same position as Mrs Carmichael, she would be expected to be grateful enough to marry him. As nice as he was, he was not above seizing the opportunity, just as this hateful man had grabbed his. 'Go ahead!' she said disdainfully. 'No one will believe you. I shall say I found the brooch, which I did—and there's nothing you can do about it,' she added defiantly. Better to deal with John than this man, she thought.

'And let you get away with it?' he said silkily. 'Oh, no. I'm sorry to disappoint you, but that's not on. I've too much respect for your womanly wiles where Sanderson's concerned. I shall hand you over to Mrs Carmichael and not to another of your besotted slaves. Where did you find the brooch, anyway?' he asked, suddenly changing the subject and catching her unawares, and she blinked as she tried to find a suitable answer. 'Considering we searched the whole house,' he went on blandly, not missing her quick look of consternation and drawing his own conclusions, and his lips twisted sardonically. 'That was a good idea of yours to leave it in the conservatory. We didn't spend over-long in there, did we? That was quick thinking on your part, wasn't it? Only I've a feeling that it wasn't meant to be found, not unless things got hot for you.'

'You can think what you like!' Rebecca retorted coldly. 'I'm tired, and I'm going to bed,' she declared emphatically, sounding a lot more certain of herself than she actually felt.

'You'll go when I say so, and not before,' Janus

said quietly. 'You haven't answered my question. Where did you find it?'

Rebecca glared at him. What a persistent devil he was, she thought, as she sought for an answer. 'I don't see why I should answer that,' she said haughtily, 'or what right you have in putting me through this third degree,' and as she said this, she moved to one side and started to make for the door. At least that was the idea, but Janus Leon had other ideas, and she found herself swung round to face him again.

This latest unceremonious manhandling of his was the last straw for Rebecca, and her hand was automatically raised to deliver a sharp slap at his handsome face in rebuke for such treatment, but she never made the contact. Her hand was caught in a vice-like hold that made her wince in pain.

'I'm not one of your admirers,' he said harshly. 'You'd do well to remember that, particularly as we're going to see a lot of each other in the future. I'm going to make you a proposition that you'll be wise to accept, unless you want to find yourself behind bars.' He gave her a wolfish grin. 'I think I can afford you now, Miss Lindsey,' he added meaningly.

Rebecca's eyes gave their reply before she said slowly, 'Are you blackmailing me, Mr Leon?'

Janus Leon's dark brows shot up at this. 'Now who said anything about blackmail?' he asked blandly. 'I do you a favour and you do me one. It's as simple as that,' he said smoothly.

'And if I refuse?' she asked, knowing the answer

full well, but she wanted to be clear about it.

He gave a nonchalant shrug of his broad shoulders. 'I should have thought that would have been obvious.' His eyes went slowly over her slight figure. 'You are attractive. I'll give you that, but I'm not interested in your vital statistics. I happen to be old-fashioned enough to look beyond a pretty face. It's what's underneath that counts. Strip you of that gorgeous wrapping and what do we have? A pushing little go-getter who happens to have light fingers. You know,' he drawled, 'I could even forget all that, it must be hard for you mixing with the wealthy, so from your point it's understandable. What I'm not prepared to overlook are your highminded views, your innate snobbery. I loathe snobs, and it's time someone pulled you off that pedestal you've put yourself on. I shall enjoy every moment of it, too,' he added harshly.

Rebecca's eyes fell away from his disdainful look, and she studied the hem of her dress. She was in a tight spot and it was too late to wish they were on better terms so that she could appeal to his sense of fair play. He was out for revenge and in no mood for compromise. She sighed inwardly, if only she could get him to take the brooch to Sir George and make his accusation to him, but if he did as he had threatened, and took it to Caroline Carmichael—she swallowed. There was a lot she was prepared to do for Laura, but there were limits. Perhaps, she thought hopefully, if she told him the whole story he would see how it was, and why it was so imperative to keep Laura's part out of it.

'Look,' she said quietly, 'I'll tell you what really

happened, and if you still want to make trouble then there's nothing I can do about it,' and she went on to tell him how she had found the brooch in Laura's room. 'She found it in the passage,' she said. 'She only wanted to annoy Mrs Carmichael. You must have noticed that they don't get on,' she added. 'There was no question of her keeping the brooch, but when there was such a hue and cry about it, and Mrs Carmichael practically accused her of taking it, which Laura rightly denied at the time, she saw how stupid she'd been, and I offered to help her get rid of it.' She took a deep breath. 'I was going to leave it in the conservatory, as I told you.'

Her eyes watched Janus Leon's expression and seeing a sceptical look appear in his blue eyes, she knew he refused to believe her. 'That's a bit low, isn't it?' he said silkily. 'Involving John's sister. Got it in for her, have you, because she doesn't see you as John's wife?'

Rebecca was back to the mad stage. She had told him the truth. The fact of the matter was that he couldn't bear to lose an opportunity of paying her out. 'Ask her!' she snapped furiously. 'I wouldn't have told you, only I had no choice. All I ask is that you keep quiet about it for Laura's sake.'

'I see,' he said blandly. 'I just go up to her and enquire politely if she swiped Mrs Carmichael's brooch, is that it?' he asked sarcastically. 'I'm not such a fool. I've no intention of letting myself in for a defamation of character suit, thank you, particularly as I don't believe a word of it!' He studied her for a long moment, then said, smoothly, as if talking about the weather, 'Now I'll tell you what I shall do. I shall "find" the brooch in the conservatory. Under the circumstances, I'm sure you won't mind if I use your idea on that,' he said smoothly. 'In return for my co-operation you will accept the post of my private secretary.' He gave her a long calculating stare. 'I've a yen for a glamorous secretary,' he added, giving her a wolfish grin. 'Like a status symbol, I guess. Some folk go for a Rolls-Royce, but my taste is a little more exotic.'

During this time Rebecca felt as though a net had been thrown over her, she could almost feel the silken strands weaving around her figure, and knew a moment's panic. He couldn't be serious, surely? Was he just enjoying himself? she wondered.

She was not long left in doubt. 'We shall travel,' Janus went on. 'Madeira for a start. I've some unfinished business there.' He gave her another of those bright stares of his. 'If you've not got an up-to-date passport, I'd advise you to get cracking and get it in order. We'll be leaving in about three weeks' time. After that, there'll be a visit back to the old country,' he went on, apparently unaware of Rebecca's stunned expression. 'Dad'll be tickled pink to meet you. That was one piece of advice he gave me in the early days,' he added, with a wicked grin. 'He told me to get myself a pretty secretary, then he'd know I'd made it.'

Rebecca's lovely blue eyes stared at him. 'You're mad!' she gasped breathlessly, and took a deep breath. 'If this is a joke, then it's gone far enough!'

she declared coldly.

His expression hardened. 'I mean every word, and you'd better believe it,' he said harshly. 'You have until tomorrow to make up your mind. Take an early breakfast. I'll be waiting,' he advised her grimly. 'If you refuse then I go to Mrs Carmichael with the facts,' and so saying, he turned and opened the door, allowing Rebecca to make her escape. 'Sleep on it,' he said hatefully. 'But don't underestimate me.'

CHAPTER SIX

REBECCA went straight to her room. She was in no mood to talk to Laura, not even to reassure her that all was well.

It might be all well with Laura, but Rebecca could hardly say the same about her own state of affairs! Through no fault of her own, she had landed herself in trouble up to her neck.

When she was in her room, she walked towards her bed and sat down wearily. How on earth had she allowed herself to be talked into doing something she did not want to do? Her smooth brow creased in a frown. Well, she had not said yes yet. She sighed. What was the use of pretending? She was going to do exactly what Janus wanted her to do. She had no choice, and he knew it. He had ended all speculation in that line when he had casually said he would hand her over to Caroline

Carmichael to deal with.

Her small hands clenched as she recalled his voice as he had uttered this threat. Almost as if he had known that that was the last thing that Rebecca had wanted, not to mention Laura, and the ensuing result of such an action.

Her soft lips twisted. He was clever; she had to give him that, as much as she disliked him. She drew in a deep breath. It was no use trying to think up some way she could extricate herself from his clutches. He had meant every word. To be strictly honest with herself, she could understand his reasoning. She had continually snubbed him that whole week, and he was not used to that kind of treatment, certainly not from a woman! He was experienced enough to know that she was not in love with John and had assumed she was only after a title and the money to go with it.

On the face of things, she must appear pretty cheap to him, she thought wearily, not that she cared what he thought about her—She frowned again. No, that was not strictly true. She did care, she wouldn't have been human if she didn't. Perhaps she was a snob, and he was right in that. It was a fact that she had never fallen in love, and had never been attracted by any man. She was much too critical, expected much more of them. In fact, the kind of man she might have loved simply did not exist, and she was most certainly not going to settle for second best.

She moved restlessly. Janus knew none of this, so it was easy for him to condemn her. She got up, and straightened her back. It was time she put

Laura into the picture. There would be no occasion
to have a quick word with her in the morning,
Laura was nearly always the last down to breakfast, and what she had to tell her was going to take
some explaining, especially after her previous
assertion that she did not care for Janus Leon. If
the news that she was going to work for him was
suddenly sprung on her the following morning, the
chances were that she would put two and two together and come up with the right answer, forcing
her to own up.

After giving a light tap on Laura's door, she
slipped into her friend's room and found her ready
for bed, but still stretched out on the counterpane
reading her paperback, and when she glanced up
and saw Rebecca, she gave a lift of her eyebrows
and asked, 'All clear on the Western Front?'

Rebecca nodded. 'It will be "found",' she said,
and sat down on the bed beside her.

Laura's sigh of relief showed that she must have
been holding her breath until Rebecca's return, and
making Rebecca glad that she had decided to call
in on her. 'What do I do?' Laura asked with a
grin, 'wander into the conservatory, and say "Hey
presto!" and produce it?'

Rebecca shook her head. 'Too obvious,' she said,
with her tongue in her cheek, because that was
probably how Janus Leon was going to play it. '*I*
should leave it for another enterprising soul to dis-
cover it—probably your father,' she added for
good measure, and at Laura's nod of agreement,
went on hastily, 'Laura, what would you say if I
told you that Janus Leon's offered me the job of

private secretary?' she asked.

Laura's eyebrows shot up at this. 'I'd say you're a lucky devil,' she said forthrightly, and gave Rebecca a hard stare. 'You're not going to refuse it, are you?' she asked with a look of incredulity. 'You are!' she exclaimed accusingly. 'Honestly,' she added with exasperation, 'what wouldn't I give for such a chance! Why—I'd take a secretarial course right now if I thought he'd wait that long,' she declared fervently, and added indignantly, 'and I think it's pretty good of him, considering the way you've given him the run-around this week.'

Rebecca's brows lifted. 'I've done no such thing,' she declared, equally indignant. 'He was only out to annoy John, anyway. And I took those notes for him, didn't I?' she finished.

'Was that when he asked you?' asked Laura interestedly. 'I'll bet you turned him down then, didn't you? He looked a bit put out, I thought, at dinner.'

Rebecca looked away from Laura and stared at the rich carpet on the floor. 'I said I'd think about it,' she lied, 'and tonight he asked me again,' this time telling the truth, only there was no asking, only telling, on that occasion.

'I see,' Laura replied thoughtfully, 'and he wants your reply before he leaves in the morning, does he? Well, what are you going to do? Take it? You'd be a fool to turn it down, you know. I suppose,' she added candidly, 'you don't fancy being chased round the office desk on the odd occasion.' She grinned. 'I told you he'd got his eye on you, didn't I? That you should be so lucky,' she ended enviously. 'I think he's gorgeous!'

Rebecca gave her a pitying look. 'I've worked for him before, remember, and there was no horse-play then. It was strictly business—I wouldn't contemplate it otherwise,' she added firmly.

Laura looked up at her swiftly. 'You've decided to take it, then?' she asked.

Rebecca nodded. 'As you said, it's a chance I can't really turn down. Especially as he mentioned travel.' She kept her eyes averted from her friend. 'I've always wanted to travel,' she added. 'I suppose,' she tacked on diffidently, 'I just want a push. That's why I wanted to talk it over with you.'

Laura's eyes shot up to heaven. 'The woman's mad!' she declared emphatically. 'Well, if you want my advice, I'd say, accept the job. Chances like that come only once. You'll only be kicking yourself if you turn it down, especially when you get back to the College and all those dull dons.'

'They're not dull!' Rebecca replied half indignantly and half amused, 'just a bit absentminded— the older ones, anyway.'

'Well, that's settled, then,' Laura said firmly, and scrambled off the bed. 'Now, off you go to bed, before I turn green with envy,' and she walked over to the door and opened it before Rebecca could say anything more, and gave her a gentle shove out into the passage.

As Rebecca prepared herself for bed, she told herself she ought to be congratulated on carrying out her mission so successfully, since there was no chance now of Laura suspecting any foul play and all she had to do was accept Janus Leon's ultimatum.

Now that it was done, Rebecca felt an odd sense of relief. She had burnt her boats, and curious as it seemed, was not in any panic over the thought.

If anything did worry her it was how she was going to explain her extraordinary turn-around in Janus Leon's favour to John, and she vaguely hoped she would get Janus's co-operation in keeping the matter quiet until she had had a chance to speak to John about it.

There was also her job at the College. Giving in her notice was not going to be easy. They would find someone else, of course, she was not vain enough to think that she was irreplaceable, but there was no doubt that several of the College intellectuals would be very put out by her leaving. They were used to her, and she was used to them, and each had their own way of going about things, little idiosyncrasies that would have to be learned the hard way by whoever took over the post.

Rebecca sighed. It might be as well if she just took off. They would have to accept someone else then, and she was not looking forward to the fortnight's training she would have to give her successor either, for she knew only too well the little tricks her learned employers would get up to to discourage the unfortunate applicant. Her mind was still busy on these thoughts when sleep claimed her.

When she awoke the following morning, she was aware of a feeling of expectation, of a lightness of heart that she had never felt before, and as she dressed after her bath, she tried to pinpoint this extraordinary happening.

On the face of things, she should have been

dreading what looked like a very uncertain future, yet deep inside of her she could only realise a sense of release. Release from a sameness that had been her life's pattern until now, and a release from the fear that she was wasting time. A fear that had been with her since Barbara's amused but accurate remarks about her cloistered existence at the College.

When she had brushed her hair, her thoughts turned inevitably to Janus Leon, and as she stared at her reflection in the dressing table mirror, she recalled what he had said about not being attracted to her.

Was it this that had decided her? she wondered, for had he shown any inclination towards a romantic dalliance with her she would have found some way out of her dilemma, although what, she had no idea, for men like Janus Leon did not make idle threats, and she was certain he had read the situation right, hence his veiled threat of giving the brooch to Caroline Carmichael, and that was the last thing Rebecca had wanted. Her soft mouth twisted wryly. Had she stolen the brooch, she would have considered herself lucky to have got off so lightly.

In spite of her earlier expectant feelings, Rebecca experienced a twinge of anxiety as she went down to breakfast, mainly on Laura's behalf in case things did not go right, and the whole wretched business was exposed.

To her surprise, she found Laura already at breakfast, an almost unheard-of state of affairs, as she, like Caroline, was always the last down, and this only increased Rebecca's anxiety, as it was apparent that she was not the only one worrying about the outcome.

This, however, was not the only thing on Rebecca's mind. There was the delicate task of giving her reply to Janus, for until she did, the brooch would not be 'found.' This thought seemed to conjure up his presence, because at that precise moment he walked into the dining room, and bade the girls a hearty, 'Good morning.'

John arrived shortly after this, and by now Rebecca was getting slightly desperate and could not see any way of communicating her reply to Janus. She could hardly announce her acceptance of the job in front of John, who would be bound to be shocked, if not absolutely furious!

It only wanted Mrs Carmichael's presence, she thought miserably, to put the cap on things. There was no possibility of privacy while she was around. Her insensitive way of intruding upon others' conversation ensured this.

While she toyed with the frugal breakfast she had helped herself to, she watched Janus and John help themselves liberally to the selection on the sideboard, and was acutely aware of Janus, and how his bright blue stare rested on her face in a contemplative manner before he turned his attention to his food.

Had Rebecca but known it, this was the lull before Laura put a spanner in the works by calmly saying to Janus as he sat down beside her, 'So you've pinched our Rebecca, have you? You wouldn't like to wait until I've gone through a secretarial course, would you?' she added hopefully, then grinned. 'Of course, I wouldn't be half so efficient as she is.'

Rebecca's startled eyes went from Laura to Janus, whose self-satisfied smile made her want to refute Laura's words, and then went to John, who had just started to tackle his food but now stared at her, his meal forgotten.

'What exactly does that mean?' he asked in an ominous voice.

Rebecca took a deep breath. She could have strangled Laura. 'I've decided to accept Mr Leon's offer of employment,' she said, adding somewhat lamely, 'I've always wanted to travel,' and left it at that.

John threw Janus a look of pure dislike, and Rebecca thought it was a good thing that Janus was leaving that morning. 'What about your job?' asked John, giving her a pleading look. 'You just can't walk out like that,' he added indignantly.

'Oh, I'll give the usual month's notice,' Rebecca said quietly, cross with John now for making life difficult for her. He had no right to tell her what to do.

'I'm afraid that's out,' Janus said firmly. 'I can't wait that long, you see. There's another four weeks yet until the start of term, isn't there? That would make it two months before Rebecca could join me, and I'm not prepared to wait that long.'

'Seems to me you've no choice,' John said jeeringly. 'Not unless you find someone else. I shouldn't think you'd have much difficulty. You're quite famous, aren't you?' he added maliciously.

Janus turned his blue stare on Rebecca. 'It seems to me it's up to you,' he said softly. 'Either you want the job or not. I need someone now, not in two months' time.'

Rebecca looked away from his searing eyes. What he was really saying was that either she abided by his terms or he would carry out his threat to expose her. In other words, she had no choice.

To Rebecca's relief, Sir George then joined them, and the conversation broke off as they returned his morning greeting, but John for one was not going to give way that easily.

'Well, that's settled, then,' he said in evident satisfaction, and smiled at Rebecca. 'You're much too conscientious to walk out of your job. You'll have to look elsewhere, won't you?' he said to Janus, giving him a thin-lipped smile.

'I say,' began Laura indignantly, 'that's a bit hard, isn't it? Rebecca wants the job. Why should she lose it because she's conscientious?' she demanded.

Sir George made his way to the table and placing his plate down on the place laid beside his daughter, asked what all the fuss was about.

'Rebecca's been offered a job by Janus, who needs help now, but John says she can't take it because she has to give notice at the College,' Laura explained caustically.

'I didn't say she couldn't take it,' John got in quickly, 'only that she owes the College some consideration,' he ended piously.

'Well, it amounted to the same thing, didn't it?' Laura retorted angrily. 'Look, Rebecca's worked for the College since she was eighteen, and that's four years, isn't it? Surely she's entitled to leave for a better job if she's offered one. What do you say, Daddy?' she asked her father, who was just settling down to enjoy his breakfast.

'Of course she is,' replied Sir George heartily as he speared a piece of sausage. 'Don't see what all the fuss is about.'

All through these exchanges, Rebecca had said nothing. She might not have been there, only Janus's bright glance resting on her now and again as if assessing her thoughts told her that even if the others seemed to have forgotten her presence, he hadn't.

'Giving in her notice,' said Laura, determined to champion Rebecca. 'Janus can't wait that long.'

Sir George finished chewing his slice of sausage. 'Still don't see that that matters,' he said, wiping his mouth on his napkin. 'They were lucky to keep her that long. We never had permanent staff in my time. Existed on temporaries, from what I can remember. Only Miss Prudence stayed,' he gave a reminiscent smile. 'Prudence by name and by nature. The temporaries brought a bit of high life into the bursary, from what I remember.'

'Same in my time, Sir George,' Janus said quickly, in a voice that plainly commended his host for taking his side.

Sir George took a sip of his coffee, then remarked to Rebecca, 'You take the job, my dear. Daresay they'll soon replace you.'

John frowned at his father, and turned to Rebecca. 'You'll do what you want, of course, but I can't see why there has to be all this rush,' and at Laura's snort of annoyance, he added quickly, 'Oh, I can understand Leon's reasoning, but you're not going to be easy to replace. It's not as if you were unhappy in your work, is it?' he said querulously.

'You can tell them she's had an offer she couldn't refuse,' said Janus with a wicked grin.

Rebecca again experienced a wish to wipe that self-satisfied smug expression off Janus Leon's handsome face. No doubt the phrase 'couldn't turn down' amused him. She also knew a sense of guilt. John had successfully touched her conscience. He was right—she had been happy at the College, and in spite of Sir George's airy comments, she felt it was unfair to just walk out of her job.

At this point a vision of an elderly lady rose before her and she drew in a swift breath of relief. Miss Johnson! Why hadn't she thought of her before? Miss Johnson had been the Bursar's secretary before her retirement four years ago when Rebecca had taken over the job, after receiving six months' training, mainly because of Miss Johnson's reluctance to leave.

Rebecca had met her several times since her retirement, as she lived within a short distance of the College, and she had made no secret of the fact that she missed the company of her college friends and found life lonely. Without a doubt Rebecca knew she would jump at the chance of helping out.

'There's always Miss Johnson,' she said quietly, voicing her thoughts aloud. 'I'm sure she'll be only too pleased to help out.'

'She's ancient!' John protested pithily.

Rebecca's eyes widened. 'At sixty-five?' she said

tartly, 'I only hope I've as much energy as she has at that age!'

The arrival of Mrs Carmichael at this point prevented any further argument from John, for her quick, 'Has it been found?' question to Sir George as she walked into the dining room brought all their thoughts back to the missing brooch, and at Sir George's sigh at having such a disagreeable subject brought up so early in the morning, and his abrupt shake of the head, Caroline Carmichael gave Laura a hard stare that made the girl send Rebecca a half hopeful yet despairing look. 'In that case,' Mrs Carmichael said grimly, 'I insist on calling in the police.'

Sir George was about to protest his feelings on the matter when Janus cut in with a smooth, 'I've been thinking. You know there was one place we didn't search thoroughly.' By now he had the attention of Mrs Carmichael, who had been about to leave the dining room in search of the telephone, and had now paused at the door. 'The conservatory,' he announced calmly. 'It's just a chance, but worth trying, don't you think?' he asked.

Had it been anyone else who had made this suggestion, Caroline Carmichael would not have listened, she was too intent on causing Sir George as much trouble as possible. Her hope of being asked to stay on at Pinehurst had not come to fruition, and she had at last come to the undeniable conclusion that whatever hopes she had nurtured where Sir George was concerned were never going to be fulfilled. In this frame of mind, she was in no mood for compromise, and more than a little spiteful, but as it was Janus who had made the suggestion, she came back into the room. 'It's nice to think that someone cares,' she said tartly, throwing Sir George a malicious look.

Sir George stood up and without a word made for the conservatory, closely followed by the rest, with Caroline bringing up the rear.

The brooch was found by Sir George a few minutes later, and triumphantly held aloft for all to see before it was snatched away from him by Caroline Carmichael, in case it vanished again.

Rebecca watched this byplay with a cynical eye. It was very clever of Janus to produce the rabbit out of the hat, in this case the missing brooch, in such a manner as to cause no suspicions whatsoever, for she had to admit that, left to her, and should it have been she who had made the suggestion to search the conservatory, Caroline's suspicions would have been aroused, particularly as she suspected Laura of the crime. Not to mention Rebecca's own doubts of being able to carry it through. Deception was not her strong point, and she felt she would have given the game away if pressed.

'It seems you weren't the only one to have that idea,' said Laura, as Mrs Carmichael all but hugged Janus, as they all settled down at the breakfast table again and Sir George rang for coffee.

Amid the general hubbub of conversation, Caroline's high voice could be heard remarking to Janus, 'But for you, I doubt if the brooch would have been found. George sees nothing but those wretched orchids of his!'

Had Sir George been fostering any regrets where Caroline was concerned, these words dispelled any such thoughts, and he sent her a look of distaste and told her that the car would be ready when she was, giving her no opportunity to delay her stay.

This all too polite offer of Sir George's brought Caroline back to a proper sense of proportion, and she tried a little too late to cover her previous lapse from grace with a girlish giggle, and asked if Sir George was trying to get rid of her, and wouldn't the car be needed for Miss Lindsey.

Before Rebecca, or anyone else come to that, could reply, Janus said casually, 'Oh, Miss Lindsey will be travelling with me.'

There was a small silence after this, while Rebecca for one digested this cool statement of his. She knew she was going to be his secretary, but had not foreseen how soon she would be expected to carry out her duties.

'Rebecca was due to spend another week with us,' John protested angrily. 'This is her holiday period, you know,' he added meaningly.

Janus, however, was not to be moved. 'I'll make it up to her,' he remarked casually. 'We're off to Madeira in three weeks' time. There'll be some work, of course, but mostly done in the sunshine.'

Whatever reply John might have given to this statement was forestalled by Laura's eager, 'Are you going to set your next story in Madeira?'

Janus shook his head. 'It's where Atlantean Studios happen to be shooting their latest film. Mine's next on the agenda. I'm going over there to vet a few hopefuls they've lined up for the leading roles.'

Laura gave a groan of pure envy. 'I don't want

to hear any more,' she declared gloomily. 'I can't bear it!'

Sir George also beat John to it by asking interestedly, 'Are you allowed to make your own choice? I thought that once they'd bought the film rights they could do what they liked.'

Janus smiled. 'I made a special point of it. They were so keen to get it that they didn't stop to argue.'

There followed a discussion on the location to be used, which would be Australia, as the story was set there, and included many scenes of the bush.

Rebecca, who had not read the book and had therefore no idea of what was required, remained silent. So did John, but the unhappy looks that he sent her while everyone else was occupied needed no verbal confirmation, and Rebecca was relieved when the company finally broke up after their delayed breakfast.

Her head felt like cotton wool, and she just nodded her confirmation at Janus's authoritative order that she should pack and be ready to leave at ten-thirty. Things were happening a little too fast for her, and she felt she could have done with a little breathing space. However, when she saw that John was preparing to waylay her, she took the coward's way out and went to her bedroom to pack, assisted by Laura, uttering groans of envy now and again, and being admonished to remember to write and tell her all that was going on.

With Laura's help she was ready in good time, and thanking Sir George for her week's stay at Pinehurst, before she was whisked into the front

seat of Janus Leon's Bentley, trying desperately to
look happy and contented, while her brain was still
reeling under the suddenness of events, and she
only half heard John's parting words that should
she ever regret her decision, she knew where to find
him. He would have said much more, but Janus
gave him no time to dwell on the matter by starting
up the motor as soon as the farewells had been
said.

CHAPTER SEVEN

As the car sped smoothly along the country lanes
that led to the main road, Rebecca stared ahead of
her, trying not to focus all her attention on the
silent man beside her, whose strong hands held the
wheel of the car.

The miles passed and to the apprehensive
Rebecca the silence was oppressive. She was well
aware that in some intangible way their relationship had altered. He was the boss and she was
a paid retainer. At least, she presumed she would
get a salary, although there had been no mention
of this since she had accepted the position. She
sighed inwardly. Considering the speed of events,
this was not surprising. No doubt Janus would find
the time to bring up the subject in the near future.

Her wide lovely eyes scanned the passing scenery.
Were they going back to his hotel, she wondered,
and would she be expected to start work straight

away? Unable to bear the silence any longer, she shifted restlessly. 'Where are we going?' she asked.

Janus shot her a look that suggested that she had broke into some private thought of his, and he replied almost uninterestedly, 'Cambridge, of course, to pick up the rest of your luggage.' He jerked his head back in the direction of the boot. 'You'll want more luggage than that. Besides, you'll have to leave your resignation, won't you?'

Rebecca did not reply to this. She was not expected to. It was plain that from now on it would be Janus Leon who gave the orders, and all she had to do was to obey them.

They reached the College just before midday, Rebecca experiencing a feeling of nostalgia as they passed the familiar front entrance and drove round to one of the entrances used by staff and tradesmen during the vacation period.

At the appearance of the lodge porter at Janus's hoot of the horn, Rebecca leant forward for recognition before the gates were opened, but old Jack Grandy, the porter, had eyes only for the driver of the car. 'Mr Leon! It's nice to see you again, sir,' he said, as he opened the gates, and only when the car passed through them into the College grounds did he see Rebecca. 'Miss Lindsey, too,' he said with a grin, then looked at Janus Leon again. 'Staying, sir, or just visiting?' he asked.

'Visiting,' Janus replied airily. 'It shouldn't be above an hour before we have to worry you again.'

'No trouble at all, sir,' answered old Jack heartily. 'Liked that last book of yours, sir,' he said, his voice showing a deep respect that Rebecca had never heard from Jack Grandy before; usually he was the most cantankerous of men.

Janus had accepted the compliment with his usual bonhomie, and Rebecca, recalling how she had gone out of her way to rebuff him the previous week, could understand why she was now in this position, and why he had wanted to get back at her in the only way he could.

She thought of the coming interviews with the likely candidates for the lead in the film soon to be produced of one of his novels. She did not know much about the world of movies, but as the film was likely to be a box-office attraction, there would be no shortage of hopeful applicants. As for the leading lady—Rebecca almost smiled as her imagination flowed on, seeing Janus besieged by a bevy of beauties hoping to influence his final decision. The stakes were high, for whoever got the part would achieve overnight success.

Her thoughts were so far away from the College precincts that when Janus eventually drew up by the entrance to the Bursar's office, she looked surprised at suddenly finding herself there, and only his abrupt, 'Well, I presume your quarters are around here somewhere,' reminded her why they were there, and she got out of the car.

'I'll be calling on an old friend of mine,' Janus told her, as he started up the car. 'I'll give you half an hour,' and before she could ask him for more time, the car swept away from her.

Rebecca walked towards the entrance of the office block, hoping that the doors would be locked and she would be unable to gain entrance to her quarters that were in the right wing of the building, but fate, it seemed, was on Janus Leon's side, for the large heavily studded doors, although closed, were not locked, and she met with no obstacle to prevent her reaching her rooms.

The bookish smell of the old building penetrated through to her rooms, and for a moment she stood in its familiar enclosure that spoke of timelessness and safety, as if nothing could change, all was as it had been, and would always be.

It was not surprising that back in the peace and sureness of the old College atmosphere, Rebecca should experience the first pangs of panic. What on earth had she done? What kind of a man had she got entangled with? What if his earlier scathing comments of not being attracted to her proved a fallacy and he took advantage of her at the first available opportunity?

She shook her head numbly in an effort to dispel this unpalatable thought. Unpalatable in more ways than one. Deep within her she knew that if Leon broke his word she would never trust another man. She did not like him, but she respected him. If she had not respected him, wild horses would not have made her place herself in his power. She would sooner have done the disappearing act until things had settled down.

For one wild moment she considered slipping out the back way of the building and making her way towards one of the other gates of the College. She was known by all the porters and would have no trouble in getting out.

On second thoughts she abandoned this idea.

She had given her word and to back out now was not to be contemplated.

Before she gave herself time to indulge in any other form of escapism, she started packing. She had waited a precious ten minutes in useless prevarication.

As the rooms were furnished, and Rebecca was not a collector of odd items, her packing consisted only of her personal belongs, and by the time the half hour was up she was closing her large case.

After one last, almost sad look around what had been her home for the past four years, she lugged her case to the door, carrying two coats over her left arm and her overnight case in her hand, wondering how she was going to manage everything in one swoop, but this was not feasible and in the end she settled for just her large case on the first trip down.

As there were two flights down to the ground floor, she did not attempt to carry the case, but placing it on the top stair, gradually slid it down from stair to stair, and this was how Janus found her in the middle of the first flight, the heavy thumps of her case enabling him to locate her.

He relieved her of the case and asked, 'Is that the lot?'

Rebecca, turning to go back up the stairs, replied, 'I can manage the rest,' and went back to collect her coats and the overnight case.

When she joined him a short time later, he had stowed her case in the back with the rest of her luggage and sat waiting in the car for her.

There was still the letter of resignation to be

written, she thought, as she climbed into the car, but that could wait until later, when she was able to produce a plausible-sounding excuse for her abrupt departure.

'I had a word with James Dudley,' Janus told her as he started up the car. 'I more or less explained what had happened.' He shot Rebecca a quick assessing look as he sensed her stiffen at his words. 'Only that I'd offered you a job,' he added softly, 'and that you'd accepted. As long as you do what you're told, that's as much as anyone will know. You keep your side of the bargain, and I'll keep mine.'

Rebecca stared ahead of her. She would never have admitted it, but those quietly said words set the seal on their association, and she felt more at ease with him than she had felt since the beginning of their strange arrangement.

They stopped at a roadside restaurant for lunch. The speciality of the house was a buffet style lunch set out on long trestles from which you helped yourself, and there was no shortage of choice.

Rebecca was not at all hungry. The events of the last forty-eight hours had momentarily removed what had normally been a healthy appetite, and she was grateful to be allowed to choose the amount of food she required and did not let Janus bully her into taking more than she felt she could cope with, ignoring his casual, 'No wonder you're so slim!' comment, as she walked back to their table with her selection.

She also refused a second glass of the potent red wine Janus had ordered, meaning to keep a clear head for whatever was in store for her. She still did not know where they would be spending the night, and in spite of her earlier relaxation concerning Janus's motives where she was concerned, this worried her, since she was aware that his suite in the London hotel had only one bedroom. The other, as she well knew, had been turned into a study. For all she knew she might be expected to doss down under the desk! It was these thoughts that made her firmly refuse to have her glass filled, and brought a pithy comment from Janus.

'I'm not trying to seduce you,' he said harshly. 'I meant what I said about not being interested in your physical attractions. You're a paid employee of mine, and I never mix business with pleasure—got that?' he demanded sarcastically.

Rebecca's wide eyes left his furious blue ones, and she stared down at the white damask table-cloth. 'Yes, sir,' she said, with a touch of humility in her voice that did not fool Janus for a moment. She raised her lovely eyes to his. 'Would you please tell me what arrangements you're making for me? I presume we are going back to the hotel?' she asked, still keeping that humble note in her voice.

Janus studied her through hooded lids. 'So that's what's worrying you, is it?' he said silkily. 'Yes, we're going back to the hotel. I shall book you a room. In time, Miss Lindsey, you'll learn to trust me. Now, are you finished, or would you like some coffee?' he demanded, and at Rebecca's shake of the head, he stood up abruptly and left her to gather her bag and coat while he settled the bill.

During the drive to London, Janus outlined

Rebecca's duties, that were not so very different from what she had been doing, only that she had to keep a diary of engagements for him. He would tell her what arrangements he had already made, and what functions he would attend and the ones he would not. He also mentioned the salary she would get, and it was much higher than she had anticipated.

Her only response to this was a slight raising of the eyebrows, and this was noted by Janus, who remarked pithily, 'You'll find you'll earn it. I'm not a slavedriver, but I do expect loyalty and hard work from you. You'll have no need to purloin any other trinkets to bolster up your dress account,' he added harshly. 'Any relapses of yours in that line, and I'll hand you over to the authorities, understood?' he added brusquely.

Rebecca's eyes flashed sparks at this very unfair accusation. He simply refused to believe that she was not a thief, and if he ever brought up the subject again she would walk out on him, no matter what the circumstances were.

He shot a quick look at her before he turned his attention to the road again. They were now on the outskirts of London, and his attention would soon be centred on the busy traffic they would encounter. 'Sore spot, is it?' he said softly. 'Okay, we won't dwell on it. Just as long as you know where you stand.'

Rebecca hardly needed to be reminded of this. She knew only too well where she stood, and the ground was far from firm.

On arrival at the hotel, Janus procured a room

for her that was on the same floor as his suite, explaining to the manager that Miss Lindsey was his private secretary, for which Rebecca received a special smile of welcome from the manager, who was obviously bent on pleasing his famous guest.

'Join me as soon as you've unpacked,' Janus said abruptly, as they left the lift, preceded by the porters carrying their luggage, and Rebecca wondered crossly if she was supposed to work weekends as well.

When she rejoined him fifteen minutes later, after she had unpacked a few necessities and taken a quick refreshing shower, she found Janus studying a bound volume, not unlike the manuscript covers, only this one had a bright red cover. On her arrival he had thrust it towards her, with a cryptic, 'Read that,' order.

As Rebecca received it, she caught the scent of aftershave lotion, and knew that he had also freshened up since their journey. His clothes were now more informal, grey slacks and white short-sleeved open-necked shirt.

'It's the script for *The Devil's Ploy*,' he said. 'Have you read the book?' he demanded.

Rebecca shook her head, and received a hard look from Janus. 'It was a best-seller,' he remarked dryly. 'You *were* cut off, weren't you?' he added silkily, as he selected a book from the shelf behind him and gave it to her. 'Read that first,' he ordered. 'Otherwise you won't understand the script.'

From all accounts, all of his books were best-sellers, Rebecca thought, recalling what Barbara had told her but she said nothing, and placing the script under her arm and holding the book in her hand, she asked if that was all he wanted, hoping to be able to return to her room, but she was to be disappointed.

'I've a few letters that need replies,' he said airily. 'They're in the desk, right-hand drawer,' he added, and looking in his briefcase, produced the notebook that Rebecca had all but thrown at him the previous day when he had first asked her to work for him.

The sight of the notebook brought back a few memories that Rebecca would rather not think about, but she placed the book and the script down on the desk and picked up the notebook, then went in search of the letters he had mentioned, and getting a pen, sat down at the desk after giving him the letters, and prepared to take dictation.

Her docile acceptance of whatever task Janus had in store for her amused him no end. It was in his voice as he dictated the replies, and only just stopped short of smugness, Rebecca thought, as she gritted her teeth and concentrated on her work.

By the time they had finished, it was tea time, and when Janus asked her if she would like to take tea in the office or have it in the hotel's dining room, she quickly plumped for the dining room, if only to give her a change of scene and possibly get out of Janus Leon's presence that she had had to put up with for most of the day.

The sardonic look she received for this choice, told her that he was well aware of her reasoning. 'That's fine,' he said dryly. 'I've an appointment at five, and won't be back until late. You've plenty to keep you busy. We'll go over the script tomorrow around ten,' he added casually.

Rebecca bridled at this autocratic order. It was obvious that he expected her to spend the evening reading his book, and the script too, unless she was very much mistaken. She was beginning to understand why he paid such a high salary. Her life, it seemed, was to be geared entirely to suit his life style. Her eyes spoke her feelings more than words could have done, and as she had no intention of entering into an argument with him, one that she was bound to lose, she said nothing, but picked up the script and the book and walked to the door.

'Had you something else in mind?' he asked silkily, as she got to the door, making her turn to face him.

'As a matter of fact I had,' she said coldly. 'I would have liked to visit a friend of mine.'

'Who?' he asked harshly.

Rebecca's brows shot up. So she wasn't expected to have a private life! Her soft lips firmed; she would have to disabuse him of that idea, and the earlier the better. 'I don't see that that's any business of yours,' she replied coldly. 'I've agreed to become your secretary, but surely even private secretaries have some time off,' she added pithily.

'Not this private secretary,' he said silkily, 'or have you forgotten our little talk yesterday evening? As for agreeing to work for me, I don't see that you had much choice in the matter, do you? You're on probation, Miss Lindsey. Now for the last time, who did you want to visit?' he demanded.

Rebecca was still recovering from his earlier comment of her being on probation, and ignoring his query, she said furiously, 'I don't intend to throw a brick through the nearest jeweller's window, if that's what you're afraid of!'

Janus's eyes glinted at this. 'Your methods are a little more subtle, aren't they?' he grated, now as angry as Rebecca was. 'No, the only time I'd worry on that account would be your attending a high-class gathering where all the sparklers would be on show. Not that you'd be so unlucky the next time, because there isn't going to be a next time. Not if you want to stay out of trouble, that is. Is this where your contact is?' he shot out at her.

Rebecca blinked. 'What contact?' she asked, her eyes wide in puzzlement.

Janus smiled grimly. 'You know, you ought to go on the stage,' he said softly. 'Someone had to turn the stuff into cash after the pieces were copied and replaced by fakes.' He blinked suddenly as a thought struck him. 'I suppose that was the real thing I took off you, was it? Or was it the fake?' Then he added half to himself, 'You knew she'd be there, and you'd probably seen it before, so you might have gone prepared for the switch.'

Rebecca stared at him disbelievingly, then took a deep breath. 'No wonder you write books,' she said scathingly. 'With an imagination like yours, you couldn't go wrong. Only in this case, you *are* wrong. Not that you'll believe me.' She took another deep breath. 'I thought I'd like to go and see Miss Basnett,' she added, thinking that if she told him the truth, he would let her go, unless he thought Barbara was the fence!

Janus frowned. 'Miss Basnett?' he repeated, then

his brow cleared. 'The agency woman,' he said.

Rebecca nodded. 'And a good friend of mine. If you think she's one of my contacts, then you're mad,' she added crossly. 'I presume you won't be needing the Bureau now?' she asked quickly, seeing the glint return to his eyes.

His autocratic look affirmed this, and he said abruptly, 'It's short notice, but you can tell her I'll settle for the month.'

That was all he said, but it told Rebecca she could visit Barbara, and she gave an inward sigh of relief as she left his suite to give Barbara a ring to tell her she was on the way to see her.

By the time she arrived at Barbara's flat, an hour later, she had rehearsed her lines well. It was not going to be an easy time for her. She had to explain why she had decided to accept the job after she had written to her and told her she had refused Janus's offer, and as soon as she had got that part of it out of the way, she would feel much more capable of managing the rest. At least she had warned Barbara about the possibility of Janus Leon taking his business away from the Bureau, so that part of her news would not come as a shock.

Barbara reacted precisely as Rebecca had thought she would. 'But why?' she had queried peevishly. 'I thought you didn't like the wretched man, now you tell me you're working for him!'

'Travel,' said Rebecca, putting the only point forward that Barbara could understand. 'We're going to Madeira in three weeks' time. Now I couldn't pass that up, could I? You said yourself that I ought to come out of the College cocoon.

Well, I've decided to follow your advice,' she pointed out patiently.

Barbara was not yet convinced. 'You haven't fallen for him, have you?' she asked sardonically.

Rebecca's face said more than words. 'Of course I haven't!' she exclaimed. 'You were right when you said he never mixes business with pleasure. I'm a walking typewriter to him, and glad of it,' she added fervently, making Barbara give her a sharp glance that reminded her to watch her words. Barbara knew her too well to be deceived. 'So all I have to worry about is taking the right clothes with me. They're making a film of *The Devil's Ploy*, did you know that? she asked Barbara, changing the subject quickly.

'I heard something about it,' Barbara replied, her mind still on Rebecca's earlier slip, and feeling that things were not quite right. 'So he hadn't given up, had he? He kept on at you to be his secretary?' she asked, reverting to the subject that Rebecca wanted to avoid.

'Well, he found out that I worked at the College,' Rebecca said slowly. 'He said more or less the same as you did about burying myself away, and I knew he was right. I don't have to stay with him if I don't like the work,' she added, thinking in terms of a long stay, even if Janus Leon looked on it as a kind of sentence for what he considered her misdemeanours, one or two years was all he could command, especially as it was her first offence. She pulled herself up sharply at this thought. What was the matter with her? He had got her thinking she was guilty now! 'Well, anyway,' she went on, 'as soon as he mentioned travel, I had second thoughts and decided to accept.'

There was a moment's silence after this while Barbara thought about it, and Rebecca followed up hastily with an offer of financial support for the Agency, and this time she was successful in diverting Barbara's attention from the subject she wanted dropped, for Barbara was delighted and extremely grateful for the offer, and accepted it without hesitation. 'I'll make you a partner,' she declared happily, 'and if you do want a change, you've only to come home. By that time we'll be a going concern. The new offices will guarantee more work.'

The conversation from then on centred on Barbara's plans for the future and Rebecca began to enjoy the visit, but thought she ought not to stay too late. She had to read the book Janus Leon had given her before the morning, and left shortly after nine for the hotel.

Back in her room in the hotel, Rebecca settled down to read the book, and it was past one o'clock before she had finished the story, but she had been so caught up in the plot that she had not noticed time passing.

As she got ready for bed, she thought about the book, and could well see why it had been chosen for a film. Set in the Australian bush, it had all the hallmarks of a thriller. In fact, she thought, it contained all the necessary ingredients for success—not only adventure, but a touch of romance, not too much to detract from the story, but enough to give an added fillip to the interest.

Her thoughts roamed as she climbed into bed, and

thought that her earlier surmises on the competition to obtain the leading roles had been correct, and she wondered whether Janus Leon had had a particular actress in mind when the film rights had been sold, for the heroine, a tall willowy redhead, might just fit one of the top actresses, Susanna Dean. Then she remembered what he had said about the visit to Madeira, and interviewing several hopefuls, and shrugged as she put out her bedside light. If Janus was as critical in his choice of actress as he was of his staff, then it might be a long session. He was not an easy man to please . . . and on this thought she fell asleep.

CHAPTER EIGHT

THE next morning Rebecca had more time on her hands. She was not due to report for work until ten o'clock, and waking at her usual time just after seven, she had ample time to study the film script before going down to breakfast at nine.

From what she could gather from the script, it kept strictly to the story. Not that she had expected anything else, not where Janus Leon was concerned. No licence would be taken with him; he was not unknown, and could afford to dictate his wishes in the matter.

Sadly, this had not been the case where other novels were concerned, for Rebecca could remember waiting to see a film of a favourite novel of hers, and had been bitterly disappointed, actually wondering several times during the screening, whether this was the story she had read, for it bore little resemblance to the actual novel.

Arriving in the dining room shortly after nine, she looked out for Janus but could see no sign of him, and presumed that he had made a late night of it the previous evening and was probably sleeping it off. This suited her perfectly, and she enjoyed her breakfast, lingering over her coffee with the pleasant feeling that she had plenty of time in hand.

When she knocked on the door of Janus's suite at five to ten, she thought she heard voices, and at Janus's sharp, 'Come in,' she entered.

The first thing she noticed was an expensive perfume that wafted towards her as she walked into the suite, and she hesitated as she heard a woman's voice coming from the room used as an office, and saw that a coat, with a Hartnell label, had been thrown carelessly across the back of the divan in the lounge, and the remains of a breakfast for two on a table near the window.

Rebecca was not a prude, but she had to admit to a feeling of shock and disappointment where Janus Leon was concerned. She had not thought him a monk, but had not expected him to entertain his lights-of-love in his suite, and what was she doing in the office? Ought she to tiptoe quietly out and wait for him to contact her when the coast was clear?

Janus provided the answer to that one as he suddenly appeared at the door of the office. 'Have you brought the script back?' he demanded, before he saw that Rebecca was holding it to her side, with the book in her other hand. 'Good,' he grunted, and waited for Rebecca to follow him into the office.

Standing beside what was to be Rebecca's desk was a tall and very lovely woman with jet black hair swept up high from her smooth forehead, and wearing a dress of deep purple that came from the same house as the coat Rebecca had seen in the lounge, then as the woman looked at her, she found herself undergoing a critical examination from her black eyes that were far from warm as she took in Rebecca's pearl grey dress with white piping, then looked at Janus, her pencilled eyebrows arching in an unspoken query.

'Miss Lindsey, my secretary,' Janus said smoothly, and turning to Rebecca, said, 'This is Isobel Archer. She keeps me up to date in the fashion line,' he added, with a lurk of amusement at the back of his blue eyes.

Isobel Archer gave him a hard look at this introduction, and looked back at Rebecca again. 'On Sunday too, darling?' she purred softly, but her eyes shot daggers at him.

'I should have said my private secretary,' said Janus. 'From now on, she'll be the one you'll contact.'

'Are you giving me the runaround, darling?' Isobel Archer asked through clenched teeth.

Rebecca fervently wished she could become invisible, but she was certain that should she walk out, Janus would demand that she stayed, so she busied herself by going to the desk and pretending she wasn't there.

'You do want those models used in the film, don't you?' Janus said softly yet warningly.

'Of course I do,' retorted the woman pettishly. 'Why else would I get up at that unearthly hour to have breakfast with you before I fly out there?' She glanced at her watch. 'Damn,' she said crossly, 'I shall have to rush now. When are you coming over?' she asked Janus, all fury gone, and a kind of pleading in her voice.

Rebecca kept her head down, reading the rest of the script she hadn't been able to finish before breakfast, and felt a twinge of annoyance towards Janus, and a little sorry for Isobel Archer. It was one thing to be told you weren't wanted, but quite another to be told so in front of another woman, whatever the rights and wrongs were.

'We should make it in about a fortnight,' Janus replied, obviously unmoved by the pleading in Isobel's voice, and then accompanied her to the door. A few seconds later Rebecca heard him say, 'See you,' and knew she had left.

As soon as he returned to the office giving what sounded to Rebecca like a sigh of relief, he asked abruptly, 'What did you think of the book?'

She raised her fine brows at this. If he was hoping for kudos then he was going to be disappointed, she thought crossly. She had not liked him much before, but after what she had just witnessed, she liked him even less. 'It was interesting,' she replied, managing not to sound too enthusiastic about it.

Janus stared at her through hooded lids. 'Just interesting?' he queried softly. 'I wasn't asking for bouquets,' he went on pithily. 'Just a straight-forward comment, and that appears to be beyond you. Still, I suppose you were rather cut off at the

College. I mustn't expect too much of you,' he added sarcastically.

Rebecca threw him a look of dislike, but said nothing and waited to begin work.

'Feeling sorry for Isobel, are you?' he asked in the soft voice that Rebecca disliked. 'If so, you've a lot to learn. Isobel's as hard as nails. She wouldn't waste time on me if it didn't suit her plans. She's left Hartnell's and is starting up on her own. I'm her ticket to success, you see,' he added dryly.

Rebecca still said nothing, but sat staring down at her desk. If anyone was hard, it was Janus Leon, she thought scathingly.

'You'll meet a lot of those in the future,' he went on. 'And I'm depending on you to keep them out of my private life.' At Rebecca's sudden look up at him, he added softly, 'I'll tell you which ones I'm interested in, not only from the business side.'

She flushed as she caught his meaning. He was welcome to them all as far as she was concerned, she thought. 'Yes, sir,' she said calmly, and almost grinned as she caught the blaze in his eyes.

For the rest of that morning Janus kept her busy on notes appertaining to the script, and a few changes he wanted to make. 'They suggested using Susanna Dean for the lead, but I talked them out of it,' he said. 'She's got a bit temperamental— knows she's a box office attraction, and plays on it. I hate temperamental women,' he added grimly. 'You might make a list of three who might be suitable. There's Dinah Casey, Shona Bredon, and Kay Phillips.'

Duly making a note of the names, Rebecca mused that the part of the hero, Richard Denby, should have taken precedence over the heroine, unless Janus had already made up his mind who would play the part.

As if reading her thoughts, he asked abruptly, 'Seen Guy Tindall or Daniel Dupré in action?'

Rebecca was not an avid filmgoer, and only made a point of going to see certain films that appealed to her, and had to shake her head.

For this she received a sardonic look. 'Well, I'm pretty sure Guy Tindall is the man for the lead. The only thing against him is his age. He's coming up for forty, although that's something that's played down, of course, and he's shown an interest.' He paused for a moment, then added, 'The other parts are settled. It's only the leads we've yet to agree. Have you got your passport in order?' he asked abruptly. 'A fortnight's not long to get it up to date.'

Rebecca thought she had told him her passport was in order, but she mentioned it again, and was told to let him have it. She would rather have held on to it, but Janus Leon was the boss, and she decided not to argue.

The following two weeks passed by quickly for Rebecca. By this time she was well acquainted with her new job. As the days passed she was not disappointed in her expectations as to the type of boss Janus Leon would be, and the kind of relationship they would share. He was the boss, and she was his secretary. Her dry observation to Barbara when she had first come to London as his secretary had proved a true one. In Janus Leon's eyes she was seen simply as a mechanism that kept his business going.

At the start of their relationship, Rebecca had

asked for nothing more, but as time went by she began to resent the fact that he treated her as a minion to do his bidding, rather than a human being with a life of her own, and views that did not always coincide with his, and the relationship being what it was, she did not express.

As the perfect secretary, she knew her place, and refused to rise to whatever bait he threw out at her when her calm demeanour annoyed him. Either he wanted a secretary or a sparring partner. Rebecca was his secretary, so he would have to look elsewhere for the other.

To say that Rebecca was entirely unmoved by her illustrious boss's machinations would not be the truth. For instance, when she had known that Isobel Archer had not spent the night with Janus on that first morning she had reported for duty, her feelings, that had at first registered a sense of disappointment and shock, had lifted unaccountably as she heard the truth.

There were many other pointers that Rebecca was not quite so immune to his presence as she made out, but of these sentiments Janus was not aware, since she was well trained in masking her feelings.

If anyone had suggested to her that she was falling in love with her boss, she would have indignantly denied any such suggestion, and if the matter had caused her any heart-searching she would have instantly recoiled from the thought. Janus Leon was no different from other men, and if she had been fool enough to fall in love with him, then there was only sorrow ahead of her. He had shown her only too well what he thought of her. She was a snob who needed taking down a peg or two, and worse than that, a thief who had no hesitation in robbing her friends.

He was also a playboy, according to Barbara, who usually knew what she was talking about where society gossip was concerned, although Rebecca had to admit that since she had started working for him, he had shown no sign of such clandestine activities, and as she was sure that he had not turned over a new leaf for her benefit, she presumed he was concentrating on the coming film and had no time for amorous adventures.

There was no shortage of invitations—some on embossed cards, and a few verbal calls from husky-voiced females, who received a shock on hearing their calls answered by Rebecca's cool refined voice, whereupon the caller's voice would get a few degrees colder as the message was given.

All these calls were duly reported to Janus, and that as far as Rebecca was concerned the end of the matter for her, as they were obviously personal calls, and it was up to him to return the call personally. There had been one or two occasions when he had asked Rebecca to give his apologies when he was unable to attend a certain function, and one persistent caller, the Honourable Sylvia Barkington-Leedway, after receiving two refusals in the space of a week, accused Rebecca of not passing on her message and demanded to speak to Janus.

'The Honourable Sylvia Barkington-Leedway,' Rebecca said quietly, as she passed the receiver over to him during the middle of a dictating session, giving him no choice but to take the call, and he shot Rebecca a furious look as he took the receiver from her.

While she bent her head to her notes, she heard Janus's smooth explanation as to why he hadn't been able to accept the invitations, and how he was caught up with work.

When he had finished, he banged down the receiver and glared at Rebecca. 'I pay you to keep such women off my back,' he said harshly. 'In future you will handle all calls. If I want to speak to the caller I'll tell you.'

Rebecca did not usually reply to this type of criticism, but in this case she felt she was in the right. 'That was the third time she's rung,' she said coldly, 'and each time I gave her your message. It seems she didn't believe I'd spoken to you and wasn't going to be put off again.'

Janus studied her. 'She doesn't usually give her full name, how did you know who she was?' he asked, suddenly changing tack.

Rebecca had not expected this question, and she had to think before she replied. 'Because I knew of her,' she said coldly. 'She's a distant cousin of the Bursar, and I recognised her voice.'

Janus stared at her and Rebecca knew that look. 'Been to any of her parties?' he asked softly.

Rebecca's brows rose. 'Of course not!' she said quickly. 'I wouldn't have been asked, and I wouldn't have gone if I had been.'

'Yet you expected me to go, did you?' he said softly. 'Well, I did go to one, not having the benefit of inside information, and I left halfway through. If there's anything more boring than a room full of half drunk idiots, I've yet to find it.' He gave

Rebecca a hard look. 'I'm surprised you passed up the chance of an invitation, it should have been easy enough to have wangled one. You could have got away with a king's ransom, and none of them would have missed them before noon the next day.'

'You could have accepted the invitation and taken me with you,' Rebecca replied, too furious to watch her words. 'It could have been my last big coup before going straight,' she added sourly.

'There'll be no more coups for you, my girl,' Janus said silkily. 'You're going straight from now on.'

Rebecca wondered what it would take to convince him that she was innocent, and decided that only a sworn affidavit from Laura would do the trick and convince him of the truth.

As if Rebecca's thoughts had reached Laura, she turned up the following day with a large box of chocolates for Rebecca, and handing them to her, said, 'I didn't have a chance to thank you properly before.'

Accepting the chocolates, Rebecca, knowing what Laura was thanking her for, wished Janus also knew, but she could hardly bring the subject up in front of him, particularly as Laura appeared to have developed a crush on him and would not thank Rebecca for putting her in an embarrassing position. There was also the chance that Janus would apologise to Rebecca after hearing the truth, and worse than that, ask her if she still wanted to be his secretary, which would put Laura into the picture and make her feel even worse.

Rebecca took the box of chocolates to her room expecting Laura to follow her, but Laura elected to stay and talk to Janus, hoping, Rebecca found out later, to wangle herself a job as assistant to Rebecca, who was, as she put it, going to be very busy, but after Janus's smooth but definite reply that he was sure Miss Lindsey could cope, she had to give it a rest. This she told Rebecca when she saw her off later.

In no time at all, Rebecca found herself packing for the Madeira visit. She had never been farther than the Continent before, and was looking forward to the widening of her horizons. The only snag being the company she was forced to keep, but then one couldn't have everything, she told herself stoically.

The four-hour trip was over too soon for Rebecca, who loved flying, and for the first time in her life had travelled first class, with all the attendant luxuries this entailed.

Certain that Janus would spend the time briefing her on more details to cover their fortnight's stay, she was pleasantly surprised when he settled down in his seat and appeared to go to sleep, although she was sure that if she had asked him a question he would have replied to it, in spite of his assumed drowsiness.

When they reached Funchal and had collected their luggage from the small airport's carousel, Janus led the way out of the airport lounge to the car park which was only a few steps outside the reception area and towards a uniformed driver standing beside a gleaming Ferrari, who took their luggage and stowed it away in the boot, after asking Janus if they had had a good trip.

As not a word, apart from the initial query about the flight, was said, it was obvious to Rebecca that this was not Janus's first visit to Madeira; the chauffeur had known him and obviously knew where they were heading, and probably wore the livery of the hotel, although there had been no badge on his coat.

Thirty minutes later they arrived at the hotel, which was situated high up on a hillside that over-looked Funchal.

The entrance to the hotel, along a long sweeping drive bordered with bright pink hydrangea bushes, gave Rebecca an idea of the sort of prices charged from what must be one of the luxury hotels of the island, and her first sight of the hotel with its sweeping lawns and fountains did nothing to dispel these thoughts.

The City View Hotel was a large white structure with blue shutters to each window, and balconies festooned with huge bronze vases that held delicate ferns that trailed down the white walls.

Rebecca took all this in with a deep breath of contentment. Her first impression of Madeira had been a disappointing one. She had expected to find an island of flowers and greenery, but the drive from the airport had shown hilly slopes with patchy sandy ridges that gave an impression of drabness and aridity, much more like a desert island than a floral gala. Nearer to Funchal, however, the flowers were more evident. Bright coloured oleanders hung from fences and trailed over any suitable hold.

As they drew up in front of the hotel, Rebecca's thoughts were on exploring the town as soon as possible. It was one or two miles from the hotel, nearer two than one, she thought, but as she loved walking, the distance did not worry her, and in spite of the fact that it would be all downhill going, and all uphill returning, she would not have entertained the idea of using a taxi.

On arrival at reception, Janus was given a warm welcome by an august personage who must have been the manager, if not the owner of the establishment, who told Janus that they had given him the same suite he had used before, and bestowed a look at Rebecca of perhaps more than the usual interest, when Janus introduced her as his secretary.

It was not until they entered the lift that Rebecca realised that she would be sharing the suite with Janus, but she decided not to complain until she had seen the size of the suite, and was glad that she had not aired her views on the matter, for it was of ample size, and could almost be called a flat, for its spaciousness. There were two bedrooms, with a study in between that would allow Rebecca some privacy, likewise a separate shower and toilet facilities to each bedroom. The lounge was large and well furnished, and there was a television set in the far corner of the room.

When Rebecca had unpacked in the larger of the two bedrooms, that Janus had magnanimously allotted her, she had to smile at the incongruity of the situation, and what Laura would have thought, or Barbara come to that, of her sharing rooms with her boss, but such was the relationship between them that she had no qualms whatsoever, in spite of that knowing look the manager had given her!

On the first morning of their stay, Rebecca had arrived in the lounge to find Janus wandering around in his dressing gown and ringing down for breakfast, and she had elected to take hers in the dining room; he might look on her as a paid minion, but she did feel

there was a limit, and if he expected her to take
breakfast with him, then he should have been suitably
dressed, she thought scathingly.

By now she was used to those mocking looks of
his that told her she had nothing to worry about—
well, she knew that, she thought, otherwise she
would not be sharing a suite with him, but if he
overstepped the mark just once, then she would be
on her way. If he didn't know that now, then he
would find out soon enough!

By the time she returned from breakfast, Janus
was dressed and had apparently had his own
breakfast, for she found him in the study reading
the paper and waiting for her appearance.

As there was still five minutes to go before the
time when he had said they would start work,
Rebecca did not hurry, and took her time in getting
out her notebook and pen, noticing that a typewriter had been put on the desk, that suggested
that this was a business visit only and she was not
going to be allowed to slack.

When she looked up from her preparations she
found Janus studying her with those very blue eyes
of his that echoed the bright blue of his short-
sleeved shirt. 'You took your time,' he drawled.

Rebecca met his eyes with a shade of annoyance
in hers. 'You did say nine-thirty, didn't you?' she
queried coldly.

He shrugged nonchalantly. 'You could have had
your breakfast here,' he said silkily.

'If you'd taken the trouble to dress, I might have
done,' Rebecca replied disdainfully.

As soon as she had said it, she knew it was a

mistake; the flash in his eyes told her so, and so did his answer.

'I do as I please,' he ground out, 'and I'm not having my actions queried by you. You're a nobody to me, just a piece of office furniture I picked up in my travels, and don't you forget it. I don't care a damn for your maidenly virtue—if that's what it is, although I doubt it. I've a feeling you wouldn't have complained if I'd had a title, or the hope of one. You're such a damn snob! Well, you've nothing to fear from me. I've told you that before, haven't I? You're welcome to any titled fool you can get—when I go back home again. Until then, watch your step,' he warned her harshly.

Rebecca kept her eyes on her book, and that was just as well, because if he could have seen the fury in them she would have been in more trouble, but her stiff, 'Yes, sir,' told him that she understood, and they got down to work.

Curiously enough, after that first flash of temper, Rebecca felt quite pleased with the way things were going. As long as Janus looked on her as a piece of furniture she was safe, and there would be no complications.

The philosophy behind these thoughts was the outcome of her childhood, had Rebecca known it, and would not have been admitted if told so. Her fear of falling in love was the main cause. As long as she was treated with contempt, her heart was safe. She was not fool enough to admit that she had lost her heart to a man who despised her. Her thoughts were the same as they were before he came into her life. It would take an exceptional man to make her change her mind.

The first few days were spent in meetings, and she lost count of the number of people she was introduced to, and as the meetings were held in Janus's suite, she wondered if she was ever to be given the chance of exploring Funchal, since only business seemed to be on the agenda, and recalling what Janus had said on that first morning before they had left for Cambridge, Rebecca felt a little peeved. There was the rest of the week, of course, and a following week to go, with the possibility of things easing up before the end of their stay, but Rebecca was not counting on it.

Even the first party they attended was held in the hotel, and even though Rebecca could re-member a face it was not so easy to place their names, and as the list lengthened she gave up trying to remember who was who.

The actors, of course, were different. As there were only five of them, three women and two men, this was not difficult, particularly as the women hung around Janus for most of the evening and were not inclined to be over-friendly towards Rebecca, seeing her as a rival rather than a secretary.

This was understandable from their point of view. The heroine in the story was a willowy red-head, and the description suited Rebecca, who was not only a willowy redhead but had looks as well. There was also the plain fact that at first sight of her standing by Janus's side they must have received a jolt where their hopes were concerned.

Whereas Janus was entertained by the women,

Rebecca was on the receiving end of much interest from the men. Guy Tindall, the hero of so many box office successes, did his best to monopolise Rebecca's attention, but she took care not to favour a particular person and divided her time between him and the other actor in contention for the lead, Daniel Dupré, whom she preferred to the older man. He was much the quieter of the two and did not set out to impress her.

The party finally broke up in the early hours of the morning, and Rebecca, not used to late nights, escaped to her room on seeing that Janus was still in the clutches of the starlets, as he had once referred to them, and appeared to be enjoying himself, but as most of the other guests had departed, including Guy Tindall and Daniel Dupré, who had reluctantly made their farewells as they had to be on the set at the crack of dawn, as they put it. Rebecca, escaping from the clutches of a balding elderly man whom she had a vague idea was a producer, left the scene, trusting the women would fully occupy Janus's attention, and she doubted that he would know that she had left. After the preliminary introductions he had ignored her, leaving her to her own devices, although several times during the evening she had felt his eyes on her— probably making sure that she did not purloin any of the jewellery the women were wearing!

After a shower, Rebecca slid into bed with a thankful sigh. If that was film life then they were welcome to it! The determinedly gay atmosphere of the party had depressed her, because it had not seemed real, and she wondered if the frantic efforts of the starlets to

impress Janus had anything to do with it. She had
expected to see Isobel Archer at the party, but there
had been no sign of her, and that meant that Janus
had not invited her, because she was in Madeira; she
had rung him up shortly after their arrival.

Rebecca shrugged as she put out the bedside
light. That was what came of chasing a man like
Janus Leon. Isobel would be sure to hear of the
party, and no matter what Janus had said about
her being as hard as nails, Rebecca still felt sorry
for her; she had not forgotten that pleading note in
her voice before she had left that morning.

Her, she thought, and several others, and turned
her mind to the three beauties vying with each
other for the lead in the film, and wondered who
would eventually get the part. Looks would have
nothing to do with it, nor would winning ways,
but only good acting. Rebecca knew enough of
Janus by now to know that he would not be influ-
enced any other way.

Eventually sleep claimed her, and she did not
awake until well after nine. She had to scramble to get
down to breakfast, noticing as she left the suite that
as yet there was no sign of her boss, and she concluded
that he, like her, had overslept, but she was not
banking on it. Late nights did not seem to affect
Janus, and she did not mean to be late for work.

It was a rush, but she made it, walking into the
office only a minute or so after nine-thirty, only to
find that Janus had left a note for her to say that
he would be out until six, and there was a tape she
could get on with.

After her rush to get to work on time, Rebecca

was furious that he had not bothered to tell her of his plans the day before. She could have had a full breakfast instead of making do with orange juice and a cup of coffee if she had known. In future, she told herself, she would go to the office first, in case this happened again, and she would now go down and finish her breakfast—and take her time about it!

When she got back to the office, it was well after ten, and she started on the tape, now in a better humour, for she had worked out during breakfast that it would not take her long to finish the tape, and from then on she had until six to please herself what she did, and a visit to Funchal was the first on her agenda.

Her fingers pounded the machine and words filled the page she was typing, and her thoughts were on the story unfolding before her. As she listened to Janus's deep resonant voice, she acknowledged that he had not lost his touch. The book was a winner and would sell as well as the others.

She wondered when he had made the tape. It must have been in the early hours of that morning, probably to make sure that she had something to do, she thought sourly. He would not like to think of her taking it easy, he was paying her well enough.

By lunchtime, she had finished the tape and was looking forward to her afternoon off. She would have lunch in the hotel first, and be off on her wanderings afterwards.

The sun was shining in a blue sky, and Rebecca, glancing out of the window at the pool below, and seeing the recumbent forms of the sunbathers, was tempted to do a spot of sunbathing herself. She could spend perhaps an hour there, and still have time for her walk.

As she was on the point of tidying her desk, the office door opened, and expecting to see Janus, she gave an inward groan when she saw Guy Tindall, and wished she had put the latch down on the door after returning from breakfast. Janus had his key, and had told her to lock up after her, if she left the suite in his absence.

'I'm afraid Mr Leon's out,' she said brightly. 'He'll be back around six,' she added.

'As a matter of fact, it's not Janus I wanted to see,' Guy Tindall replied in that rich deep voice of his that had earned him so many admirers. 'I didn't think you'd be still slaving away,' he added loftily. 'I hoped to find you at a loose end. How about dinner with me this evening?' he asked, giving her a smile that would have melted any other female's heart but Rebecca's.

She tried to look regretful. 'Sorry, I'm a working girl,' she said, softening her refusal with a smile. 'Thanks for asking me, anyway,' she added, as she picked up the sheets of the typed manuscript in a manner that suggested that she was very busy.

'I thought the age of slavery was over,' he said with a wry twist of his lips. 'No one, but no one, works in the evenings, not unless there's a rush on. Okay, how about this weekend? And don't tell me you work weekends as well. We can go to a party I've been invited to, or just have a quiet dinner somewhere, if you prefer it.'

Rebecca did not intend to give way, even if her boss approved of her accepting a date with the man who was probably going to get the lead in the film. She was looking forward to some time on her own, and had to repeat what she had said before about her being a working girl, and at the beck and call of her boss.

To give him credit, Guy took her refusal with good grace, but he threatened to have a word with Janus about the way he treated his secretary, and to ask his permission to take her out. With these words he took his departure, much to Rebecca's relief.

After a light lunch, she went back to the suite and changed into her bathing suit, then putting on a light skirt and a button-down blouse over it, and collecting her sunglasses and lotion, she made her way to the pool and settled down in a shady spot near the water on one of the lilos provided by the hotel. The shade was necessary, as it was very hot, and Rebecca did not intend to go down with sunstroke and be left to the tender care of Janus Leon.

As the afternoon drowsed on, Rebecca, who could feel the rays of the sun through the leafy cover of the tall trees that formed the barrier between the hotel and the steps that led down to the beach proclaiming that this was private property, felt so relaxed that she decided to stay and let the world go by. The thought of going back into the hotel and changing again to go down into the town did not appeal to her; besides, it would be after six by the time she got back, and for all she knew, Janus might want some work done, and would be in a foul mood if she was missing.

Having convinced herself that she ought to stay put, Rebecca gave herself up to her sunbathing, and let the warm rays of the sun sink through to her recumbent body.

After tea by the pool, she went back to the suite, giving herself plenty of time to have a shower and change, ready for her boss's return. By now she knew that when he gave a time he kept it, providing he was not held up somewhere.

Just before six, and with an inward feeling of relaxation, she went to the office to wait for Janus. As she had presumed, he was on time, and when he strode into the office she was at the desk awaiting orders, but instead of work, she found herself undergoing a third-degree concerning Guy Tindall's visit. The actor had apparently wasted no time in carrying out his threat of talking to Janus.

'How long did he hang around up here?' Janus demanded.

Rebecca blinked at the sudden question. 'Oh, not long,' she replied crossly, feeling like a child being questioned by her father.

'Well, I'm glad you didn't encourage him,' Janus said abruptly. 'And if you get any more wolves hanging around, let me know. I suppose Daniel Dupré will be the next one to try his luck,' he added grimly.

Rebecca could have screamed, but said nothing. She had liked the younger man, he had not been at all pushing in his manner and had not set out to impress her in any way.

'Prefer him to Guy Tindall, do you?' Janus asked softly, reading her thoughts with an accuracy that no longer surprised her.

'As a matter of fact, yes,' Rebecca replied frankly. 'I did prefer him. I thought he was a much more natural character,' she added emphatically.

'It wouldn't be because he's the third son of an earl, I suppose, would it?' he sneered. 'Guy Tindall has no such illustrious parentage.'

Rebecca drew in a deep breath. He was accusing her of being a snob again! 'I didn't know where either of them came from,' she said icily. 'But it proves my point, doesn't it? Breeding does count,' she added meaningly, not caring whether this upset Janus or not, she was tired of being unfairly accused.

Mad was not the word. He was furious, and he caught her wrist in an iron grip. 'Still regretting not landing John Sanderson, are you?' he said silkily. 'Settle for a third son, would you? I suppose there's always the chance of an early demise for the two elder ones. One word from me, and he wouldn't touch you with a bargepole, madam, so watch your step!' he advised her grimly, and releasing his hold, pushed her towards the door. 'I've got a date tonight, so I'll not need you until the morning. Don't leave the hotel,' he warned her harshly.

When Rebecca had reached her room, she drew in a shuddering breath. She had only envisaged working for him, but had not seen herself under house arrest wherever she went, and her first reaction to Janus's order was to disobey it. If she went for a walk there was no one to stop her, she told herself, providing Janus had left for his date, and if he was still in the suite when she left, she could always say that she was going down to dinner.

To while away the time until Janus had left, she walked over to the window and looked out at the midnight-blue sky gleaming with countless stars.

Ahead of her she could see the dark outline of a hillside with tiny twinkling lights that denoted homes built on the hill, and she drew in a breath of wonder. It was like a fairy land, and would have been so much more appreciated had she been happy, but her last encounter with Janus had taken away all appreciation of the finer points of life.

He had chosen a fine time to revert to the past, she thought wearily, just as she was beginning to think he had forgotten it, and just because he thought she was showing an interest in someone. She knew she ought to have held her tongue, but he had provoked her. By now, she thought, she ought to be used to him, and stay away from topics that annoyed him, but as far as she was concerned, he disliked her to the point of turning any topic to her disadvantage. Whatever views she held were, as far as he was concerned, biased by snobbery.

When they got back to London, she would contact Laura and ask her to tell Janus what really happened that night. The danger as far as Caroline Carmichael was concerned was now over, and she did not intend to spend the rest of her time shackled to the side of such a man, Rebecca told herself stoutly. She could depend on Laura, particularly if she saw a chance of taking over from Rebecca, for she knew that she would keep her word and take a course of typing and shorthand, fired by what she considered was Rebecca's stroke of luck.

A glance at her watch told her that dinner was now being served, and collecting a light wrap to put over her shoulders, she picked up her shoulder bag and left the suite without encountering Janus, and presuming that he had left for his date, silently wished him a good time, for that would put him in a better mood the next morning, then, feeling like a pupil playing truant, she skirted the dining room passage and made her way to the foyer and freedom.

CHAPTER NINE

TAKING care to avoid the numerous taxis that swept into the drive of the hotel, taking guests out for an evening of pleasure, Rebecca left the hotel grounds, and coming out on to the main road to the town, she noticed that there were plenty of taxis cruising around in the hope of picking up passengers, their bright green tops with black bodywork made them easy to spot at a distance, and she thought fares must be cheap with so many of them plying for trade. She thought of the busy streets of London and what a time she and Barbara had had in trying to get a taxi, and having flagged one down only to find someone nearer grabbing the taxi before they could get to it. She must remember to tell Barbara what the service was like in Madeira, she thought with a smile.

Ahead of her lay the town's twinkling lights, and on the other side of the road as she went down the hill, were the brilliantly lit entrances of other hotels. Above the town, the hills that she had seen from her bedroom window gave the same panoramic view, only on a wider vision, the bright twinkling lights looking like stars against the dark outline of the hills, and again she experienced that sense of wonder, tinged with sadness.

Tearing her eyes away from the hills, she saw a small park on her left, with a lake, the area clearly defined by soft lighting, that showed a black swan regally patrolling its boundaries, and as she moved into the enclosure, she noticed several more now on the farther banks settling down for the night. There were seats dotted around the lake, and bright flowers set in borders gave it a peaceful setting.

From beyond the lake ahead of her she could see more twinkling lights, and after accustoming her eyes to the view, she saw that she was looking at the harbour which lay farther down the hill. She stood for a few moments silently taking in the peace and tranquillity around her, then reluctantly turned back to the road again. She might not get another chance to explore the town, but if she had an hour or two to spare she could always find this place again.

Farther down the hill, on the opposite side of the road from Rebecca, lay yet another hotel, its drive illuminated enough to be able to highlight the comings and goings of the residents, and where the drive began, she saw a couple embracing, and drew an inward breath. The man reminded her of Janus Leon, although his back was towards her, and his height prevented her from recognising the woman. Just then they turned towards her, and she saw that she had been mistaken in the identity of the man as the couple clasped hands and walked towards the town.

Rebecca walked on, not really understanding why she should have mistaken the man for her boss, and if it had been him, it was no business of hers what he did. That was what the sensible side of her said; the other, sentimental side, had known great relief and a lightness of heart, but she was not going to listen to that side. If she was getting sentimental and stupid, then it was the island that was at fault, not her, she told herself sternly. Once back in London she would find this to be so, and would be fervently glad she had not made a fool of herself over someone who thought her a nobody, and as he had so nicely put it, someone he had picked up on his travels who was useful as a piece of office furniture.

Rebecca felt better after these thoughts. She was back to disliking the man again, and this was the way she preferred things.

So engrossed in her thoughts had she been that she had not taken in the fact that she was indeed falling in love with Janus Leon, and that was what all good secretaries did, providing the boss was handsome and single, and had devastating charm when he cared to use it. All this she would have to admit one day, when the danger was over, until then such admissions were out of the question.

By now there were many more people about, some passing her and others on the road ahead, and as Rebecca looked down the hill, she noticed that she was passing through an avenue of trees that led the way to the outskirts of the town, and giving them a closer inspection, she saw that they bore a blue blossom that reminded her of a type of wisteria, and again she wished she would be able to see them in daylight. She certainly had not noticed them on the way to the hotel when they had arrived.

By now she had reached the town, and in front of her, in the middle of a crossroad, stood a ring of fountains on a grassy verge, with a border of flowers and a type of privet shaped into large balls at intervals around the centrepiece. It would look refreshing enough in the daytime, Rebecca thought, but now, with lights playing on the cascades of water, it enhanced the scene.

Rebecca stood looking at the fountain, content in the knowledge that she had not got to rush anywhere, but as her view became partially obscured by people who had passed her, she gave her attention to a small shop on the other side of the road, and she crossed to get a closer look at the wares exhibited in the windows, and spilling on to the pavement to attract attention.

Gazing into the windows, she took stock of the gifts offered for sale. There was the usual collection of straw hats, numerous small porcelain figures, and working the pesetas back into pounds she found they were on a par with the prices back home, but on the whole most of the gifts were good value for money. A small galleon finely worked in filigree in a gold-coloured metal caught her eye and she thought of Barbara and Laura, who she was sure would appreciate such a gift, and wandered into the shop, only to find a queue of customers waiting to be dealt with, all taking their time in choosing their souvenirs.

While Rebecca waited for her turn, she looked around the shop and saw some beautifully embroidered blouses and lovely tapestry work. She knew that the embroidery would be expensive and though she would have liked to have bought herself a blouse, she resisted the temptation. She might be earning good money at the moment, but there was always the chance of an abrupt end to her employment. Recalling what Janus Leon had said about her services not being required when he returned to Australia, and the film scheduled to be made there, and was the next on the agenda, Rebecca foresaw an end to the association in the not too distant future.

By the time Rebecca had been served, she had to admit to a feeling of tiredness, that was not surprising, considering the very late night, she had the previous evening, and after hearing someone say, 'Oh, I can't trail all up there,' after being told that the item she required could be got in the town's main shopping area, she decided to head back to the hotel and have an early night. There was one more week, she told herself, and surely she would get another chance to explore Funchal, probably starting out earlier than she had today, and as a taxi slowly passed her, she hailed it, and was back in the hotel by eight-thirty.

As she entered the suite, she was looking forward to a shower and the luxury of an early night, but she had got no farther than the lounge when the telephone rang, and as she answered the call, she wondered if it was Janus checking up on her, and if he had rung before.

Her relief on finding that it was not Janus, but Daniel Dupré, soon turned to exasperation as she learned that he wanted to see her, and was in the lobby of the hotel, ready to dash up at her word,

and she fervently wished that she could think of a
good excuse as to why she couldn't see him. To
just say bluntly that she wanted an early night
might sound impolite, and she had no quarrel with
Daniel. On the other hand, she did not want to annoy
Janus, but Daniel's quick and apologetic, 'Look, I
won't keep you long. I want to ask a favour of
you, and it's nothing to do with Janus,' eventually
persuaded her to see him, and a few minutes later
she was opening the door to his knock.

'I do apologise,' he said, as he entered the suite,
'but I'm in a bit of a hole,' and he waved the brown
paper bag he was carrying in the air, then sitting
down at Rebecca's invitation, explained the reason
for the visit. 'All I want you to do is to keep this
for me until tomorrow evening,' he said with a
beguiling smile. 'I promised a friend of mine I'd
look after it for him—it's a surprise, you see, and I
can't keep it with me as I'm sharing with the local
gossip. If I walk in with this, he won't rest until he
knows what's in the bag, and the cat will be among
the pigeons,' he grinned boyishly. 'I'll not only lose
a friend, but take a dive in my career, if it gets
out,' he added ruefully, as he opened the bag and
drew out an impressive-looking jeweller's box that,
had it not had the jeweller's name on it, might have
been taken for a cakebox. He then opened the box
and withdrew a beautiful tiara that flashed and
twinkled as the light caught its brilliant stones.

Rebecca's eyes opened wide as she stared at the
tiara, and looked back at Daniel. 'I think it ought
to go in the hotel safe,' she said firmly.

Daniel chuckled. 'Looks good, doesn't it? But

it's not the real thing, you know. It's a stage prop, believe it or not.'

Rebecca found this hard to believe. Stage prop or no, she thought she knew good stones when she saw them, for they were not paste. Her eyes showed her disbelief.

'Honestly,' he said earnestly. 'Look, the real thing would weigh a ton, wouldn't it? These are synthetic stones, and the band is only plastic.' He placed it on Rebecca's head to prove his point, and as she had to acknowledge, he had spoken the truth; the tiara was no weight at all.

She was about to confirm this when Janus walked into the lounge, and after her first startled glance at him, quickly snatched the tiara off her head and pushed it at Daniel.

'Been shopping, have we? You did do well, didn't you?' he said silkily.

Daniel opened his mouth, then closed it again, aware that Janus was furious, and tried to work out why, then grinned sheepishly, 'I was just asking Rebecca to keep it for me until tomorrow evening,' he explained.

Janus's growled, 'Yes?' was not very encouraging, but Daniel ploughed on. 'It's old Wainwright's, you see. Well, not actually his. He's had it made for Helen. She's being a bit awkward about playing the Duchess again, said she refused to stagger around with the original prop—er—the tiara, I mean, so Wainwright had this one made up. It's as light as a feather. I was just showing Rebecca,' he hesitated, and Janus glared at him, reminding him that he hadn't finished the story.

'Well,' he went on hopefully, 'he's sharing a room with her, so he couldn't put it anywhere where she wouldn't find it, and it's got to be a surprise. I'm kipping in with Arnold Ashton, and he's the town crier, apart from having a nasty habit of throwing himself at any parcel that might contain food. He's got the appetite of a goat! If I walked in with this,' he indicated the box on his knee, 'he'd give me no peace until he knew what it contained.'

There was a small silence after this, and Rebecca stole a glance at Janus, who she could see was having trouble in accepting the explanation. He's wondering whether we've teamed up, she thought angrily, and he's surprised us inspecting our haul.

After a tight-lipped nod of acceptance, Janus took responsibility for the tiara, not giving Rebecca a chance to take it back to her room, and after a few more desultory remarks about things in general, Daniel took his leave, still not sure why Janus should have displayed such antagonism towards him. He would work it out, Rebecca thought ironically, and come up with the wrong answer, putting it down to jealousy where she was concerned.

When Daniel left, Rebecca's hopes of an early night were very quickly dashed by Janus's curt order to get her shorthand book, he wanted to get things finished this end, since they would be leaving Madeira the next day.

Rebecca, collecting her book from the office, knew a feeling of relief that they were going back to London, but this was tinged with a regret that she had not seen much of Madeira, and would have seen even less had she not slipped out earlier that evening, and again recalling what Janus had said about it not being all work, she had to make an effort not to show her feelings when she joined him in the lounge.

After taking several notes, she found that Janus's 'date' had been with the studio, making the final selection of the heroine. 'We did the scene where the plane comes down in the bush,' he told her, and Rebecca's mind went back to that chapter. The pilot, she recalled, had been unconscious, and the girl playing the part of a model was dressed in a creation that was meant to give the first preview of the fashion house delights in store for the waiting photographers at the airport they were due to land on, had a freak storm not thrown the plane off course, forcing a landing through shortage of fuel.

Rebecca could quite see why this particular scene had been chosen to prove the actress's ability to act the part of a girl who only knew city life, and had heard gruesome stories of the bush since her childhood, and now found herself not only in the dreaded area, but with an unconscious man as her companion.

'Dinah Casey, definitely over-acted,' he commented bluntly, 'and Kay Phillips made the scene look like a day trip out to the zoo. Shona Bredon's the one for my money. She'd just the right approach. It's not easy,' he commented dryly, 'to look bewildered and terrified at the same time, but she managed it. There was no altercation, we all felt the same way, so that's settled,' he added on a satisfied note.

After taking a few more notes, Rebecca was

allowed to have her belated early night, with an authoritative order from Janus to pack her things that evening, as they would have to take pot luck on a flight back, and it might be an early one, he warned her.

As it happened he was right, and they left Funchal on the nine-forty flight, having had a last-minute rush to the airport, with Rebecca promising herself to go back there at the earliest opportunity, and take her time in exploring the island in her own time, and not at the beck and call of her imperious boss!

Back in London, Rebecca settled down to her duties. The new book was coming on fast and she was kept busy, although she did manage to see Barbara, now installed in her new premises, and feeling pleased with life, for business had picked up, and she had no worries moneywise, in fact, no worries at all, and she looked forward to the time when Rebecca would join her as her partner in a working capacity, and not a silent one.

Rebecca had mixed feelings about this. It was nice to know she had somewhere to go, but she could not work up any enthusiasm over the project. She felt unsettled, in spite of the work Janus was giving her, and supposed it to be the visit to Madeira that had caused it.

By now she was used to Janus's ways, and he to hers, and they worked well together, and if the truth were told, she did not want to change anything, but she knew that when he decided to go home, she would have to start another job, either with Barbara or somewhere else, preferably somewhere else, she was not cut out to be a business tycoon, and needed work that was challenging and would keep her occupied. She also knew that she was in love with Janus, and she half hoped for, yet dreaded, the parting of the ways.

Once she had made this admission to herself, she felt calmer, and did not fight her feelings. He would never think of her as anything else but an efficient secretary, who might be easy on the eye, but had a lamentable way of collecting other folks' belongings, specialising in jewellery. No wonder he would be only too pleased to dump her when the time came!

With thoughts such as these in her mind, she got a shock about a fortnight after they had returned to London, with Janus announcing that they were off to Australia in a fortnight, and she had looked at him with wide eyes. He had said 'we', hadn't he? she asked herself.

'It's not all bush,' he had said sarcastically, on noting Rebecca's reaction to the news. 'Some parts are quite civilised,' he added harshly.

Rebecca flushed under his sardonic look, but her thoughts were elsewhere. He had meant her, too, she thought wildly, but why, after he had made it quiet clear that she could please herself what she did after he had left? Without realising it, a tiny hope sprang up in her heart, but she quenched it immediately, for that had been another surprise, the depth of her feelings for him, now that he was supposedly going out of her life. She swallowed. She had to know. 'Why?' she asked bluntly, completely ignoring his earlier comments, and there was nothing in her face to show how much her heart was beating.

'Why?' repeated Janus, with a lift of his left eyebrow. 'I should have thought it would have been obvious. I'm not going to stop writing, you know. I need you, and I can't be bothered to go through the motions of finding someone else, not after having trained you to my satisfaction,' he added bluntly.

Rebecca felt a spurt of anger. She hadn't expected anything else from him, but the cool blunt way he had answered her query had made her hackles rise. If he had said the wilds of Borneo, she would have been expected to follow him without a murmur—or so he thought.

'For how long?' she asked. She did not intend to get stuck the other side of the world without any means of getting home.

Janus studied her through narrowed lids. 'Does it matter?' he enquired silkily.

Rebecca wanted to stamp her foot in temper, but refrained from doing so. 'Of course it matters!' she answered furiously. 'It's not like going over to the Continent, is it? I might not like Australia, and it's a long way to come home, and you did say you would have no need for my help once you left England for good,' she reminded him coldly.

'Who said it was for good?' he countered. 'Right now I have no option but to go home, my father's been under the weather and needs some help. If I don't go he'll overdo things, as he did once before.' He drew in a breath that told Rebecca that he was having difficulty in keeping his temper. He had expected her to fall in with whatever he wanted, and had not foreseen any difficulty. 'Look,' he said

slowly, 'I've said I need you. We've yet to finish
the book, haven't we? All things considered, I just
won't have time to look around for a replacement.
When things settle down again, I promise you I
won't hold you back if you want to go home, after
the book is finished, that is. I shall of course pay your
fare,' he added on a dignified note, that suggested
that if she thought otherwise then she had misjudged him, and she ought to have known better.

Rebecca took due note of the fact that he had
not threatened her with what he considered her
failings, and the reason why he had forced her to
work for him, which was just as well, she thought
darkly, for she would not have hesitated to contact
Laura and get things straight once and for all.

As these thoughts went through her mind, she
saw that Janus was watching her closely, almost
willing her to accept the terms. She shrugged. She
had nothing to lose, she told herself. He would
keep his word, she knew that, and there was still a
long way to go in the book, but with any luck it
would be finished within a month or so, providing
Janus got down to it and did not get bogged down
on other business. With a curt nod, she accepted
his terms, and noting his sigh of satisfaction,
realised that she really had had no choice in the
matter, not as it was put to her, and that was typi-
cal of Janus Leon!

There was no further discussion on this subject,
apart from his getting Rebecca to send a cablegram
to his father, telling him when he would be arriving,
now that their flight reservations had been made.
'That will make him ease up,' he had said to

Rebecca when the telegram had gone.

Once that was out of the way, Janus concentrated on the book with a fervour that made Rebecca wonder if they would make such headway that her stay in Australia would be of short duration, although she wouldn't put it past him to have the next one already mapped out in his mind, and expect her to carry on in spite of what he had said earlier, but in her heart she knew she would go as soon as possible. Eventually he would marry, and it would be an Australian girl, probably someone waiting for him to settle down after his travels. She knew he was pleased at the prospect of going home, for he had occasionally reminisced on the past, and how he was looking forward to taking up old acquaintances, and how she would get on with this person or that, and Rebecca said nothing, and kept her thoughts to herself, often thinking how blind he was, and without knowing it, cruel, for she could play no part in the future he was mapping out for himself, apart from the office equipment. He did not actually say so, but according to her observations, she was sure that he had decided to go home for good, making perhaps the odd journey abroad when necessary.

By the time the fortnight was up they had got to within three chapters of the finish. By now Rebecca could gauge this, for Janus always kept to the same amount of chapters, and her suspicion of him already having the next on ice ready to start at the end of the current book were confirmed, and it seemed a long way to go to finish the book, but she knew that if she were to comment on this, he would be furious. She had agreed to go with him, and that was the end of the matter as far as he was concerned.

On the morning of their departure, Rebecca chose to wear her latest acquisition in the dress line, a dark blue pinstriped suit, complete with shirt and tie, a feminine copy of a man's suit, with a navy blue soft felt hat, that also echoed the trilby. She knew that the climate they were going to would still be cool, as it was not quite spring in that part of the world, and Janus had warned her to pack warm clothing.

As she picked up her shoulder bag and her overnight case, she took one last look round her room to see that everything was tidy and she hadn't forgotten anything, which was unlikely, for she had had plenty of time to pack, and as she left the room she found herself hoping that the same arrangement could be made where they were going. It had been nice to have her privacy again, and to feel a person in her own right when she had left Janus's suite for the day, on hand, of course, should he need her, but able to escape into her own world when he didn't.

Janus was just leaving his suite as she arrived, and his blue eyes went coolly over her ensemble, then widened. 'Good gracious!' he exclaimed.

By now Rebecca ought to be used to his criticism, but as usual, it irritated her and she pulled her hat further down on her head. 'You said to wear something warm, didn't you?' she replied disdainfully.

Janus did not reply but stood staring at her until Rebecca could stand it no longer. 'It's the fashion,' she said crossly.

'I know,' he answered, with a twinkle in his eye. 'I saw a similar model in Isobel's collection. You look like a gangster's moll!' he added in a pained voice, and stared down at his grey pinstriped suit. 'I feel I ought to rush out and buy a homburg in keeping with things, you know.'

Rebecca did not deign to answer this, but swept towards the lift carrying her handbag. Their luggage had been taken down earlier by one of the porters, and her head was as high as her temper. Not only did he criticise her views, but her clothes now, she thought, and had a momentary spasm of panic. What on earth was she doing setting out for the other side of the world with him? She ought to have her head examined!

It was not too late to back out, she told herself as the lift carried them down to the ground floor. She could excuse herself in the airport lounge and make a break for it, couldn't she? Janus had to take that plane and would have no time to look for her.

As they walked through the foyer, Rebecca noticed two women wearing similar outfits to hers. One was a short, stout woman who obviously should not have attempted to carry off such a style, and the second one, a rather elderly woman, though slim, wore the suit in an air of defiance against femininity in any shape or form, but in spite of these lamentable examples, Rebecca felt justified in her remarks that it was the fashion, although she doubted that Janus had seen either of them. He was probably working out his next plot, she thought dryly.

To her surprise, she found she had misjudged him, for as they climbed into the car that was taking them to the airport, he commented dryly. 'At least you can wear it,' and as he settled himself beside her in the car, he said, 'It's okay, I guess, but don't wear it in my father's presence—he'd have a fit. He's got old-fashioned ideas where women are concerned!'

Rebecca's brows lifted. He had almost given her a compliment, then spoiled it by bringing his father into it, but she had to admit the outfit was certainly not office wear.

By the time they had bought what magazines they wanted for the long journey, and had a cup of coffee in the V.I.P.s' lounge, Rebecca had forgotten all about her earlier wish to walk out on him, and if the subject had been brought up, she would have replied that she was looking forward to the trip. She would never get the chance again to see 'Down Under', at least not for free, and with the knowledge that she could come back when she wanted to, she would have been a fool to miss the opportunity. There was more to it than that, but she was not admitting it!

CHAPTER TEN

BY the time the plane touched down in Sydney, Rebecca never wanted to travel again, in spite of travelling first class, where the lounges were

spacious, and the ladies' room almost a lounge in itself. She had never travelled this far before, and was
suffering from the well known malady of 'jet-lag'.

To please Janus, in case his father should decide
to meet them at the hotel, she had changed into a
tweed suit with a matching coat in colours that
echoed the Highland heather, and worn with a lilac
jumper, looked more in keeping with Mr Leon's
idea of women's dress.

Janus's approval was evident as she joined him
for an aperitif in the lounge after freshening up,
and trying to collect her bemused senses now they
were back on terra firma.

'Guess he's got held up,' he commented, referring to his father. 'We'll give him ten minutes or so
before we order, in case he's made arrangements
for us to dine at his place. Are you hungry?' he
asked Rebecca.

She shook her head. The journey had appeared
to be a succession of food and little delicacies to break
the monotony of the flight, and she could cheerfully have waited until breakfast for her next meal,
she thought, as she sipped her drink that was supposed to give her an appetite, and if she was expected
to sit down to a meal, she only hoped it worked.

When Janus had told her that he had booked
her into the hotel for a day or so while he looked
around for more permanent accommodation, she
had at first felt a rush of relief. To be in his constant company had been of no help at all where
her heart was concerned, and to see him only in a
business capacity would have been far better for
her. On the other hand, she had experienced some

disappointment, for she had felt certain that the
house in the story he had written on her first
acquaintance with him had in fact been his home.
The picture he had drawn had seemed too real to
be a fictional object. It could, of course, have been
a place he did know well, a friend's home perhaps,
but Rebecca could not rid herself of the notion
that it was more personal than that, but all the
facts seemed to point away from such a deduction.

Janus's father was not a farmer who would own
such a homestead, as Rebecca had subsequently
found out from Janus's remarks on the flight out. He
was, in fact, a very successful stockbroker, now a widower, and spending most of his time in a flat in the city
which could accommodate Janus, but not Rebecca.

There had been a large establishment on the
outskirts of Sydney where the family had lived for
many years, but when Janus's mother had died,
and Janus had chosen a writer's career that took
him away for long periods at a spell, there had
been talk of selling the property, and Mr Leon had
moved into smaller premises nearer his work.

'Does he know where to find us?' Rebecca asked,
as it had suddenly occurred to her that the hotel was
in the city and some way away from the airport.

Janus gave her a look that said 'Really!' then
remarked casually, 'I rang up his office and left a
message.'

Rebecca nodded; of course he would have done
that. They had arrived two hours ago, and after
unpacking a few things she had stretched out on
the bed and lost count of time for an hour. Perhaps
that was what was wrong with her, she thought,

she had not got her bearings yet. 'Jet-lag,' she murmured, almost apologetically.

Janus nodded complacently. 'You'll be fine to-morrow,' he said, then looking towards the entrance of the lounge, said, 'Ah, here's my father,' and standing up went to meet the tall and unmistakable likeness of himself, whose brown hair now showed streaks of grey at the sides, and in a minute Rebecca was shaking hands with him.

Apart from the colour of the eyes, for Mr Leon's were brown and Janus's that startling blue, Rebecca knew she was looking at a replica of what Janus would look like in thirty years' time. If he had his father's courteous manner and quiet composure, then no more could be asked, she thought, but it appeared that he had inherited his artistic talent from his mother, who had had a penchant for writing poetry.

As soon as the subject of dinner was brought up, Mr Leon had promptly replied that they were having it at Rosings, and Rebecca presumed this to be a friend's home, since it did not sound like a block of flats.

'Do you mean to tell me you didn't sell after all?' Janus asked in surprise. 'I thought you said you'd put it on the market.'

Mr Leon looked a little abashed, as if caught out in some misdemeanour. 'Well,' he began, then smiled, 'I did put it on the market, and the first applicant wanted it. I guess I hadn't really got that far in my mind, and when it came to the crunch, I couldn't do it. I'd always hoped that one day——' he left the sentence unfinished, but it was plain what he was referring to. Then he coughed. 'There was Lily and Frank to consider, too,' he added. 'They're getting on a bit, and not old enough for retirement. Anyway, there it is. I was never really sure what you thought about my selling. I knew you used to be fond of the place,' he ended slowly.

If he had ever been in doubt on this score, Janus's face gave him the answer, and echoed the pleasure he felt at the news. 'That's great!' he smiled, and turned to Rebecca. 'Can you get packed up?' he asked. 'There's plenty of room at Rosings, and with Lily and Frank around, there's no worry about accommodation.'

Feeling as if she had never stepped off the plane, Rebecca went to her room to pack again, thanking providence she had not unpacked much and would be ready in no time at all.

With Janus at the wheel of the car, and Rebecca and Mr Leon in the back, Rebecca was aware of a few surreptitious glances from Mr Leon while she was taking in the scenery, as they headed for the outskirts of Sydney, and his, 'So you're a secretary,' took her by surprise, for she would have thought that Janus would have made this quite clear.

Before she could answer, Janus said in an amused voice, 'He thought you were the lead in the film.'

So that was why he was curious about her, Rebecca thought. He was probably worried that his son was becoming involved with an actress. It was a sad but true fact that these marriages rarely lasted, particularly if the wife insisted on carrying on her career. She drew in a quick breath. Why should she presume he was thinking of anything to do with marriage?

The talk then turned to the forthcoming film, and Rebecca was pleased to hear Janus comment that he did not intend to supervise the whole show. He would see cuts every now and again, but was perfectly satisfied with the producer, and they had the best director, so he foresaw no hiccups.

By this time they had reached the suburbs, and now and again passed large houses, set in their own landscaped gardens, the upkeep of which, Rebecca thought, would cost a small fortune.

Another hundred yards or so and they turned into a tree-lined drive and just around the bend, hidden by bushes, lay the house.

It was small wonder that Mr Leon had considered selling it, Rebecca thought, for it was a large house that would have several more rooms than the usual home.

As the car drove along the drive, Rebecca, taking in the scenery, thought that if you did not know where you were, you could be forgiven for thinking that you were back in the U.K. The house was no different from many to be found in the higher price bracket at home, and the dark evergreen bushes that made up the borders lining the well kept lawns, that would shortly be ablaze with colour when the spring began, were no different from their counterparts all those miles away.

Soon the car was drawing up in front of the stone pillars of the entrance to the house, and Rebecca found herself in a cool hallway tiled in mosaic style, that would give a refreshing welcome from the hot summer sun in the days to come. Ahead of her was a wide ornamental staircase that gave an impression of the size and elegance of the rooms it led to.

Mr Leon opened a door on the right of the hall and stood aside for her to precede him into the room, which was a large lounge comfortably furnished. 'Lily will be busy with the dinner,' he explained with a smile, as he walked over to a miniature bar at the end of the room. 'What do you fancy as an aperitif?' he asked her.

'Nothing, thanks,' Rebecca replied, taking the comfortable chair that Mr Leon had indicated. 'To tell you the truth, I'm not really hungry either,' she went on, wishing she could be taken to her room and just lie down.

Mr Leon gave her a sympathetic grin. 'It's a long way,' he said, 'but you'll get your bearings soon enough,' he added confidently, as he carried two glasses of what looked like whisky, and putting one on the table near an armchair, presumably for Janus, who had wandered off towards the end of the hall and into a door on the left, he settled himself in the next chair to Rebecca, and seeing her glance at the empty chair next to the drink, he added, 'Janus has gone to make his peace with Lily—she didn't hold with him forsaking the home front for foreign parts,' he chuckled. 'Not that he'll have any trouble, she'll be so glad to see him, she'll forget the rest.'

While they waited for Janus, Rebecca found herself undergoing a lighthearted questionnaire on

her past, how she came to work for Janus, what
she did before she became his secretary, what ties
she had in England, asked with a genuine interest
that took away the feeling that she was being
vetted, although she knew she was, but she liked
Janus's father, and if this was to be her work base,
and where she would be in constant contact with
the family, it was understandable that he should be
asking these questions.

By the time Janus joined them they were on the
subject of Cambridge, and as Mr Leon himself had
studied there, there was a lot to talk about, had
they not been interrupted by Janus's, 'Dinner's
about to be served,' announcement, as he picked
up his drink and took a sip, before leading the way
to a door off the lounge, and stood waiting for
Rebecca, who had hesitated in the hope of being
let off and allowed to seek out her room, and
though she was certain that he knew precisely what
was in her mind, she had no choice but to join
him, and his amused, 'There's plenty of time to
catch up on the time lag, and you're not expected
to have a farmhand's appetite,' comment made her
wish she could hit him as she sat down at the
beautifully polished round table in the middle of
the dining room.

To Rebecca's way of thinking the table, large as
it was, seemed amply provided with food already.
There were small dishes of seafood, wafer-thin
slices of toasted bread and other small portions of
delicacies for starters, that Rebecca left strictly
alone. She would have enough trouble coping with
the first course, and she wished Janus had let her

off the hook, and as she watched the men help themselves to the starters, Janus choosing a slice of toasted bread, with what looked like cream cheese on it, she took a sip of her white wine, glad to have something to do, and partake in some way.

A few minutes later an elderly woman carrying a tray and dressed in a dark green uniform with a crisp white apron, and followed by a man of about the same age, and whose face was so deeply tanned that it was obvious that he spent the greater part of his time in the open air, and was probably the gardener doubling as butler and handyman when necessary.

As they carried the trays to the table Rebecca, noting the dark blue suit of the man, had a suspicion that they had dressed up for her benefit, and knew a feeling of embarrassment, for she was sure both of them would have been more comfortable in what was their normal wear. She fervently hoped that this state of affairs did not last long, for their sake as well as hers.

'Meet Lily and Frank Abbott,' Janus said airily, 'two true blues from Down Under whom we couldn't manage without,' he added with a grin, that was answered by a smile from the normally stern features of the woman, and by a much wider grin from her husband as they set the trays down on the side table and started to place plates of lobster salad in front of everyone, then gave their attention to Janus, although both looked at Rebecca. 'My secretary,' Janus supplied carelessly, adding, 'She doesn't eat enough, but I'll leave that to you, Lily,' and at Rebecca's indignant glance at him, tacked on, 'She'll be let off tonight, on the grounds of tiredness.'

Rebecca thought this was an odd introduction. He had not given her name, but just said she was his secretary, but then she remembered his earlier call to the kitchen quarters, during which he had probably told them her name. Not that it mattered, she thought dryly. She was his secretary and had no other pretensions.

Rebecca might not mind this casual introduction, but Janus's father obviously did. 'Which room have you given Miss Lindsey?' he asked Lily, giving Janus a reproving look, that was met with a slight raising of the brows by his son.

'The old guest room, the one with the sitting room,' Lily replied promptly, adding with a softening of her features as she turned to Rebecca, 'You'll be more comfortable there, miss. The study's on the same floor. All nice and handy, like,' she added.

Rebecca almost gave a sigh of relief. It was nice to know she would have a bolthole to retire to should Janus do any entertaining. 'Thank you,' she replied, her relief clearly showing in her voice, and producing an ironical gleam in Janus's eyes.

'Good!' said Mr Leon. 'Well, directly after dinner I suggest you take Miss Lindsey up so that she can get settled in.'

Rebecca threw a grateful look at Mr Leon. At least he knew how tired she was, she thought, and her thoughts showed as she met Janus's eyes.

'Poor little Rebecca,' he said, in answer to that look. 'Not homesick already, are you?' he taunted sarcastically.

She looked away from the challenge in his eyes.
'Of course not!' but she felt a tiny prick at the back
of her eyes that had nothing to do with home-
sickness. Why did he have to be so hard on her?
She knew it was tiredness that was making her
weak, but all the same, he could have shown some
understanding, couldn't he? she thought, as she
stared down at the salad in front of her. She could
no more eat that than fly straight back home, but
chance would be a fine thing.

She heard Mr Leon tell Lily and Frank that they
could manage from now on—in other words, they
were to leave them to it. She heard the door close
behind them, then there was a tiny silence before
he addressed Rebecca. 'Look, it's obvious you're
ready for bed. Leave that. Lily will understand.
Ask her to bring you up a nightcap,' he added
kindly.

Rebecca needed no second bidding and was out
of her chair and heading towards the door before
Janus could put his oar in with another sarcastic
remark and then she really would burst out in tears,
but she wasn't going to get away that easily, as she
found Janus beside her when she reached the door.
'Lily's still busy with the dinner,' he said abruptly.
'I'll show you up.'

If this was his way of apologising for his earlier
remarks, Rebecca could have done without it, and
she silently followed him up the grand staircase
determined not to show him how wretched she felt.
Tomorrow, she thought, she could take it, but not
tonight.

As if sensing her feelings, he left her at the door

of the small suite. 'Nine-thirty breakfast,' he said breezily, 'then work, my girl. You won't have time to moon,' and left her.

With barely a glance at the cosy little sitting room she had walked into from the hall, Rebecca went through to the bedroom, and passed a small toilet suite complete with shower on the way, cut off from the bedroom by a bevelled glass door, but she was too tired to appreciate the fact that she would have plenty of privacy. All she wanted now was to collapse into bed and sleep the hours away. Soon she was undressed and into her night-gown, and she never remembered climbing into bed; the rest was just automatic.

At nine o'clock the following morning, she was awakened by Lily, who had brought her morning tea and placed the tray down on the bedside table. There had been no need to actually wake Rebecca, for she was a light sleeper and had awakened at the almost apologetic light knock Lily had given before entering the bedroom.

She sat up in bed and sipped her tea as she watched Lily draw the curtains back, letting the pale sunshine float in the room, and saw with relief that she had abandoned that stiff uniform she had worn the night before and now wore a flowered overall, and as she walked back towards the bed, and saw that Rebecca had finished her tea, she offered to pour her another, with a smooth comment that she had plenty of time. 'We say nine-thirty breakfast,' she told Rebecca, 'but it's only a strict rule when Mr Leon or Mr Janus have to be in the city early, and there's no rush today.'

When Lily had taken the tray away, Rebecca considered whether to take her time, or whether to be prompt at the table, in spite of what Lily had said, that implied that whatever she chose to do would be all right. That was Lily's view, she thought dryly, and it would not be her boss's view, not if she knew Janus Leon, she thought, and throwing off the bedclothes, she got out of bed and made for the shower.

Ten minutes later, refreshed, not only by a good night's sleep but an invigorating shower, Rebecca went down to the dining room to find Janus and his father just about to sit down, and thanked her lucky stars that she had made the right choice. She was a working girl, not a pampered guest as Lily had implied, and she answered their 'Good mornings' with just the right shade of deference, although Janus's had been an absentminded one, probably working out the next step in the plot, she thought, as she sat beside him at the table.

The smell of eggs and bacon drifting up from the cover of the serving dish Lily carried in as soon as they were seated reminded Rebecca that she was hungry and would do full justice this time to Lily's cooking.

The conversation was desultory at first, with Mr Leon waiting until Rebecca had finished her breakfast and was on her second cup of coffee before sounding her out about a sightseeing tour of the city at the earliest opportunity, which was agreeable from Rebecca's point of view, but not Janus's, who seemed to take umbrage at his father's arrangements for Rebecca's amusement. 'That will have to wait,' he said tersely. 'We've some work to get through first. There's plenty of time for that sort of thing. It's not as if she was off next week,' he added firmly.

Rebecca caught Mr Leon's puzzled glance at his son, and saw the light shrug he gave as if to say it was beyond him, but he could not resist asking, 'Weekends, too?'

Janus gave a shrug in reply, and his abrupt, 'Very probably,' showed his impatience at the question.

Now that that subject was dropped, Rebecca was left alone with her thoughts, Janus and his father discussing the subject of the film to be made, during which she learnt that Guy Tindall had secured the leading role, something that Janus had omitted to tell her, and after his finding Daniel Dupré in Rebecca's company that evening, complete with the tiara, this was not surprising, for in spite of the plausible explanation Daniel had given, Rebecca was sure that Janus had had his reservations on the matter, and was taking no chances of Rebecca being encouraged to slip back into bad habits!

No sooner was this thought in her mind than another followed swiftly. Janus had made it quite clear that Rebecca was there in the capacity of a secretary only, and had no intention of things getting out of hand, such as her being mistaken for a likeable trustworthy person to be treated as one of the family, and recalling his harsh, 'Don't leave the hotel,' order in Madeira, she wondered what steps he would take to keep her under observation now that they were in his own home.

Rebecca studied her coffee cup with its fine gold band round the rim, but her thoughts were far away and the conversation between Janus and his father went on unheeded by her. It would not take long for the book they were working on to be finished, she told herself, and come what may, she was getting out. No way would Janus persuade her to stay, and in the present conditions he would surely be glad to see the back of her. He could not have thought things out properly, she argued silently. It was different in a strange country, when it was reasonably easy to keep a check on her, but it was different here, and as time went on could become positively embarrassing for both of them.

She felt better when she had made her mind up. She must have been living in cloud cuckoo land to have hoped for better things. There would be no trouble in getting away. Janus had given his word, and no matter how furious he was, he would keep it.

When she glanced up, she saw that both men were looking at her in an expectant fashion, and she realised that she must have been asked a question but had been too full of her thoughts to know what it was, and apologised swiftly, asking for it to be repeated.

'Sometimes it takes a couple of days,' Janus remarked with irony, meaning jet-lag, Rebecca knew, and she flushed. 'I asked if you were ready for off,' he said. 'I want that book finished.'

Rebecca wanted the book finished too, and she was only too pleased to follow him out of the dining room and up to the study.

During the morning there were several telephone calls. Word, it seemed, had got around that Janus was back, and the following day brought a lot of post, most of it invitations to this or that function.

There was another embarrassing interlude that morning at the breakfast table when Janus and his father took a hurried glance through the mail, with Mr Leon commenting lightly that Rebecca would get plenty of parties in—or didn't she go to parties? he challenged Janus.

This time Rebecca was alert, and got in quickly, 'As a matter of fact, I don't. I'm not a bit social, I'm afraid. Give me a good book and I'm happy.'

Janus nodded his approval of this declaration, and abruptly changed the conversation to a lecture he was being asked to give to the Rotarian Society, and Rebecca drew a sigh of relief. That was one hurdle out of the way. It was a question of marking time until the book was finished, and then it wouldn't matter.

It was going to seem odd, of course, with her making tracks for home after only a fortnight, when she envisaged the end of the book, but that was Janus's worry, he'd have to think up something, and with his imagination she had no doubt that it would not strain his brain power. It was a pity, she thought, that she had told his father that she had no surviving kinfolk back in the U.K., but there could always be a trusted friend who needed help, she told herself.

Now that Janus had declared his intention of settling down at home, his father had officially retired from the city, taking his doctor's advice that it was time he eased up a bit, particularly in his profession, where constant vigilance was the keynote to success or failure, but until now he had made no final decision, because he had needed work to keep him occupied in what must have been a lonely private life.

So the days passed, with Rebecca fully occupied with work, but never forgetting her resolution to leave, once the book was with the publishers.

There was a slight difference now in her working area, in that meetings were confined to other venues, which Janus would attend, leaving Rebecca at the home base, ensuring that it stayed a home base and not an office address. This state of affairs suited her, since there was no point in her becoming envbroiled in other matters other than the book work. It also ensured that she would not be included in any social affairs resulting from the renewal of old business acquaintances, who would have felt obliged to invite her to various social functions.

She might have been content to leave matters as they were, but it was plain to see that Mr Leon was not. He was not only perplexed, but exasperated by what he would have called their strange relationship. For Janus to bring Rebecca all that way, and then expect her to live the life of a recluse, solely for his own benefit, was an unthinkable state of affairs, and she knew he was keeping a watchful eye out for any indication which would explain such a state of affairs.

Had Rebecca been an older woman, or even a plainer one, an answer might have been forthcoming, but she was young and, there was no denying, good-looking enough to have caused a stampede among the young bloods if let loose on the community. These thoughts inevitably pointed to only one conclusion, as Rebecca had known it would, hence the watchful eye kept on them during the evening meal, or when Janus had a spare evening at home, but all too often, sadly from Mr Leon's point of view, Rebecca would retire to her rooms leaving the men to their own devices, and this was right, she felt, since Janus was kept busy during the day, while Mr Leon pottered around the house, devoting his time to hobbies so long neglected, and such an evening provided both father and son with time to catch up on news and perhaps a few reminiscences that Rebecca could take no part in.

If she hoped that Mr Leon would leave well alone, she was due for a disappointment, for realising that his tactics of vigilance were getting him nowhere, he decided on another course of action, which he tried first on Janus, by hinting broadly one evening that as he had a free evening why didn't Janus take Rebecca to see a show? and Rebecca, after her first annoyance at Mr Leon's obvious tactics to get to the root of the matter, found Janus's bright blue stare on her challenging her to dare to accept, for his father's benefit only, she knew, and she went into her party piece about having to get down to writing back home—she had put it off long enough, she explained with a smile that took what might have been considered a snub out of the reply.

With one down, and one to go, Rebecca was not surprised during taking tea with Mr Leon the fol-

lowing afternoon, when Janus had gone to another
business conference, to find herself on the end of
what might be considered personal questions, such
as how had a girl with her looks managed to escape
the matrimonial net. Did she have something on
the male of the species? because if she did, she must
remember that one could not class them all in the
same category—and a little more on these lines,
showing Rebecca he had come to the conclusion
that she had been badly hurt in the past and did
not intend to trust another man.

He was partially right, she thought ironically.
She did not trust men, and particularly his son,
not that there was any fear of him getting in any
way sentimental over her, for where she was concerned the damage had already been done. She
would look at no other man, but that was nothing
to do with his father.

She drew in a deep breath. There was no help
for it but to get things straight once and for all, for
in a matter of days the book would be finished and
it would look odd if she suddenly announced her
departure without some explanation. 'I'm not
intending to stay permanently, Mr Leon,' she said
quietly, seeing the way his brown eyes showed his
surprise. 'You see,' she added carefully, 'when your
son first approached the matter, we were in the
middle of this latest book, and he had no wish to
change secretaries at that stage. He was also hoping
I would agree to work for him permanently,' she
smiled. 'I'm a good secretary, you see,' she added
bluntly, 'but however much I enjoyed working for
him, I wasn't prepared to commit myself to per-

manent work so far from home. It was agreed that
I should give it a try and should I decide to stay,
all well and good, but if otherwise, then he was
perfectly agreeable to my returning home.'

It was a long speech, and Rebecca saw that Mr
Leon was having trouble in accepting the bare facts
of the matter, let alone sending all his calculations
up in smoke. 'You're homesick?' he asked bluntly.

Rebecca had a job to stop her feelings coming
out into the open, but she managed it and nodded,
then managed to smile. 'Stupid, isn't it?' she said
in a light voice. 'I've no family, as I told you, but
there's several good friends I've got left.' She met
his sympathetic look squarely. 'Under the circumstances, I mean the terms I came under, I shall be
leaving in about a week. When the book goes to
the publisher,' she ended firmly.

'But you've seen nothing of the country!' Mr
Leon exclaimed in a shocked voice. 'Not even the
city, and I'm going to see that you do. As soon as
that book is off I shall arrange some tours for
you—personally, that is,' he added grimly, 'as my
son apparently hasn't the time. Don't worry about
any business agreement. I feel it's the least we can
do. Just promise me you won't dash off on the
first plane out,' he said emphatically.

'What have I done now?' Janus's smooth voice
came from the door by which he stood. His voice
was light, but his eyes were sparks of fury as they
met Rebecca's startled ones, and she wondered how
long he had been standing there, certain that he
had not just arrived.

'If you don't know, there's not much point in

my telling you,' muttered his father, 'and I thought I'd got a bright son!' he went on in a hardly audible voice as he marched out of the lounge.

Janus looked at Rebecca. 'Study,' he commanded grimly, and turned towards the stairs with a purposeful step, confident that Rebecca would automatically follow him, which she did, but it was touch and go until she realised that she might as well get it over with. She was leaving, and there was nothing he could do about it, and she hoped his father would excuse her from keeping her word about staying for the sights!

On arrival in the study, she braced herself for the storm to come. Something on the lines of would she be good enough to inform Janus of any decision that concerned the office work, before discussing it with anyone else, etc, etc; but no such cutting statement was issued. He just pointed to her desk and sat down at his desk, to all intents and purposes ready for work, and this was another surprise for Rebecca, since he rarely dictated in the afternoon, not the book anyway, replies maybe to letters he had received that day, but after a three-hour session in the morning on the book, she had never known him do an afternoon session, certainly not as late as this.

'You want the story finished, don't you?' he said harshly, in answer to her look of surprise when he started dictating.

This produced an ardent nod from Rebecca. She had never wanted anything as much as that, at any time in her life.

'Right, then,' he said sarcastically. 'Let's get on with it.'

After this rather abrupt order, Rebecca did not find it easy to concentrate. Her thoughts were racing about in her head, personal thoughts that had nothing to do with the story. He was making sure she did not change her mind, she told herself, he had wanted her to go and was not going to miss this chance offered him.

All through these speculations, her pen was as busy as her mind, but she did not miss a word, she was too well trained for that, and her query when given a word she had never heard before was spontaneous, and what she had done on countless occasions, and Janus had taken time off to confirm it and usually to spell it out to her, but this time he showed no such politeness and snarled, 'What the hell does it sound like?'

Rebecca's brows raised at this uncalled-for remark, then she considered it, determined not to let him rile her into a fight, not when things were going the way she wanted. 'A sort of boomerang?' she suggested hopefully.

'I should have thought that would have been obvious,' Janus sneered, 'considering where we've got to in the plot.'

Still she did not take the bait. 'Only you could have said boomerang, couldn't you?' she asked patiently, 'and not used the native word.'

Janus gave her a look through narrowed blue eyes, then ran a hand through his chestnut hair in a distracted manner. 'Now I've lost the trend of the story!' he shouted. 'See what you've done!' he accused her.

'Never mind,' Rebecca replied mistakenly soothingly. 'With a local secretary this kind of thing won't happen.'

'And neither will anything else!' Janus exploded, then slammed down the book he had made some notes in. 'It's no go!' he said furiously. 'And how the hell I'm expected to concentrate under these conditions is beyond me. With this pressure it will take another six months,' he darted a sidewise glance at Rebecca. 'You promised to stay until it was finished, didn't you?' he demanded.

Rebecca gave a curt nod. If he thought she was going to hang it out, or let him do so, just because he was too lazy to break in another secretary, then she wasn't having any. Her eyes met his. 'I promised, and I'll keep it. We've barely a chapter left, and going by normal routine, two days should do it,' she said.

'There's nothing like a loyal secretary,' he said sarcastically, then glared at her. 'I should have thought you owed me more than that,' he added meaningly.

That was not going to work either, Rebecca thought with a tightening of her lips. 'Haven't you forgotten something?' she asked. 'You promised I could go if I wanted to when the book was finished, didn't you? Well, I'm going,' she stated flatly. 'It's not,' she added furiously as she made for the door, 'as if I applied for the job in the first place!' and she swept out.

'If you think I'm going to settle in the U.K., then you can think again,' Janus shouted after her. 'We're staying, do you hear?'

Rebecca heard, everyone in the house must have heard, but with a different kind of impact. She was past caring, she only knew she wanted out, and her bleak eyes met Mr Leon's twinkling ones as he passed her in the passage, and she felt a deep sense of outrage. What did they care about her heartbreak? She meant nothing to them.

'I've heard better proposals,' said Mr Leon, with a wide grin. 'As an author you'd think he could do better than that, wouldn't you?' and he passed on his way chuckling.

Rebecca stood frozen in her tracks. What had he said? Something about a proposal? What had Janus shouted out as she left? Something about staying here and not in the U.K. He hadn't meant—he couldn't have meant—She shook her head. She wasn't going to be taken in by that, and straightening her back she made her way to her room.

Something like a whirlwind passed her before she had got to the door, and that something was a six-footer with the light of battle in his blue eyes, who swung her round to face him. 'Did you hear what I said?' he demanded unceremoniously.

'You don't have to shout!' Rebecca answered, just as furiously. 'And you'd better go down and put your father out of his agony. He thinks you've just proposed to me—said something about thinking you could have made a better job of it!' she ground out.

Janus bundled her into the room and shut the door behind them with a purposeful-sounding click. 'He's dead right,' he said with a twinkle in his eyes, 'but it's not easy proposing to an ostrich with its head in the sand, and you've had yours firmly embedded in that position since we first met, plus a label round your neck that clearly stated, "Do not disturb". I didn't know whether to pull you out or entice you out. No matter what I tried, it didn't work. One thing I knew for certain was that if I made any advances you'd run for cover like a fox looking for a hole with a pack of hounds about to descend on him.'

There was a small silence after this, and Rebecca kept her eyes turned away from him, still not believing what he had said.

'I don't know why you're afraid of emotion,' Janus went on, 'but I know you are, and I'm pretty sure it's nothing to do with anything that's happened to you personally. Perhaps one day I'll find out. You can't go on running for ever, and I don't intend to let you. I'm also pretty sure that the same sparks that light me up when you're around are playing just as much havoc with your emotions, only you refuse to acknowledge it. I could have waited for ever, but as you've probably noticed I'm a bit short on patience, particularly where my personal needs are concerned. I'm asking you to marry me, tomorrow if possible, the day after, if not. What I'm trying to say is, I do not intend to wait for what's considered an appropriate period. After that,' he stated magnanimously, 'you can do as much sightseeing as you want with either Dad or me as escort, but you're not going out on the town without my ring on your finger that will tell any interested male that you're booked for life!'

Rebecca was not allowed to reply, even if she had something to say at that point, and whatever she might have thought of was vanquished under a heartstopping kiss that seemed to go on for ever, and the sparks Janus had mentioned were not only twinkling away but positively ignited as she answered the call of his ardent lips.

A short while later, after she had smoothed her hair, and tried to look calm and collected when they went down to confront Janus's father with the news—confirmed, that was—she did think of something, and without looking directly at Janus, for he had not been too keen to break it up, and she had only just managed to get her thumping heart under control, let alone smooth her hair, she said lightly, 'I didn't take that brooch, Janus.' She did look at him then, and was surprised to see a wide knowing grin on his face.

'I know,' he said smoothly, one arm starting to encircle her waist. 'Laura gave me the lowdown. I pumped her for it,' he added, as his arm clamped her to his side.

Rebecca stared at him while she digested this calm statement, then tried to pull away from him. 'You knew the whole time!' she exclaimed furiously. 'And you blackmailed me——'

Janus had no intention of losing out now, and shamelessly used force to gain victory. 'All's fair in love and war,' he whispered in the ear of his love after reducing her powers of concentration in the time-honoured way.

When Rebecca was allowed to bring some order to her rather dishevelled appearance, ready to present herself to her future father-in-law, who must by now be in a fever of impatience, they went to join him in the lounge, Janus keeping a firm hand on Rebecca's, just to make sure she was not overcome by nerves and did not try to make a bolt for it; he knew her a little too well to take any chances.

No such thoughts were in Rebecca's mind, and no fears either. Her ghosts had been laid, she had forgotten that it takes two to make a marriage work, and she loved Janus enough to take a chance on the future—although chance was not the right word, for Janus loved her, and the thing she had wanted most in the world was hers for the asking.

'About time, too!' Janus's father said gruffly, as he embraced his daughter-in-law-to-be, then he gave Janus an appraising look, that plainly said, 'Well done!' Then he said casually, 'I suppose you want a message sent to Jake out at Goolie telling him to go on a walkabout?'

Janus grinned, and laid a hand on his father's shoulder. 'How did you know?' he asked, then turned to the bewildered Rebecca. 'It's our farm,' he explained. 'It was my uncle's, I used to spend a lot of my boyhood there, and I'll give you one guess where we're spending our honeymoon!'

By now Rebecca had the answer, and knew exactly what the homestead would look like. Janus had described it all that time ago, hadn't he?

THE MAGIC OF ORCHIDS

In Jane Corrie's *Man with Two Faces,* Sir George has a passion for orchid growing. And perhaps Sir George is so taken with orchids because of the flowers' unique, almost magical loveliness.

There are thousands of different kinds of orchids—no one has been able to count them all. But it is the beautiful flower of this exotic plant that makes it so famous. Some plants have flowers a foot long, while others have tiny clusters of little jewels, each blossom no bigger than the period at the end of this sentence. The fragrance of some species can fill an entire room. It is a common belief that orchids come from jungles. In fact, they grow all over the world—in deserts, jungles, mountains and even in the tundra above the Arctic Circle.

The orchid craze began in 1818 when an English horticulturalist named William Cattley received a shipment of plants from Brazil. The rather strange foliage used as packing material interested him; he potted the bulbous roots and a short time later was rewarded by gorgeous lavender blooms with purple markings. Named after Cattley, the blossom caused a sensation among the wealthy, who paid enormous sums for a single plant. Today, the Cattleya orchid is still the most popular blossom for corsages.

Orchids make the perfect corsage not only because of their beauty, but also because they are long lasting. Some species bloom for months at a time. Even cut and arranged in a corsage, orchids can be preserved in a refrigerator by being stored on a layer of waxed paper in a plastic container. They will stay fresh for up to two weeks, and their beauty can be enjoyed again and again!